W9-AWF-994

Support the
Lucky Family
Orphanage

Lucky
Family

The Year of the Fortune Cookie

AN ANNA WANG NOVEL

by Andrea Cheng

illustrations by Patrice Barton

Houghton Mifflin Harcourt
Boston New York

Copyright © 2014 by Andrea Cheng
Illustrations copyright © 2014 by Patrice Barton

All rights reserved. For information about permission to reproduce selections from
this book, write to Permissions, Houghton Mifflin Harcourt Publishing Company,
215 Park Avenue South, New York, New York 10003.

www.hmhco.com

The text of this book is set in ITC Berkeley Oldstyle.

The Library of Congress has cataloged the hardcover edition as follows:
Cheng, Andrea.
The year of the fortune cookie / by Andrea Cheng ;
illustrations by Patrice Barton.
p. cm.
Sequel to: Year of the baby.
Summary: Eleven-year-old Anna takes a trip to China and learns more
about herself and her Chinese heritage.
1. Chinese Americans—Juvenile fiction.
[1. Chinese Americans—Fiction. 2. Identity—Fiction. 3. Intercountry
adoption—Fiction. 4. Adoption—Fiction. 5. China—Fiction.]
I. Barton, Patrice, 1955– illustrator. II. Title.
PZ7.C41943Yf 2014
[Fic]—dc23
2013024155

ISBN: 978-0-544-105195 hardcover
ISBN: 978-0-544-45592-4 paperback

Manufactured in the United States of America
DOC 10 9 8 7 6 5 4 3 2 1
4500514608

"Where I'm From" © 1999 by George Ella Lyon.
Reprinted by permission of author.

To Xinzhe
—A.C.

To Ling
—P.B.

PRONUNCIATION GUIDE

Happiness - *Xing fu (shing fu)* 幸福

Hello/How are you? - *Ni hao (nee how)* 你好

Fine - *Wo hen hao (wo hun how)* 我很好

Lucky Family Orphanage - *Xing yun jia ting gu er yuan*

　　(shing yun jia ting gu are youan) 幸运家庭孤儿院

Foreigners - *Wai guo ren (why gwo ren)* 外国人

Grandma (dad's mom) - *Nai nai (nie nie)* 奶奶

Grandma (mom's mom) - *Wai po (why po)* 外婆

Thank you - *Xie xie (shay shay)* 谢谢

Come - *Lai (lie)* 来

No problem - *Mei wen ti (may wen tee)* 没问题

Little Sister - *Mei mei (may may)* or

　　Xiao mei (sheow may) 妹妹　小妹

I'm full - *Chi bao le (che bow le)* 吃饱了

Fruit - *Shui guo (shway gwo)* 水果

Meat - *Rou (row)* 肉

Noodles - *Mian tiao (me en tee yiao)* 面条

Friend - *Peng you (pung you)* 朋友

China - *Zhong guo (jung gwo)* 中国

Chinese language - *Zhong guo hua*
        (jung gwo hwa) 中国话

Beijing - *Bei jing (bay jing)* 北京

Baby, *also* treasure - *Bao bao (bow bow)* 宝宝

Snow - *Xue (shwe)* 雪

Courtyard Houses - *Hu tong (who tong)* 胡同

Strawberry - *Cao mei (tsao may)* 草莓

A little - *Yi dian dian (yee dien dien)* 一点点

Good luck - *Hao yun (how yun)* 好运

Child - *Xiao hai (sheow hi)* 小孩

Be careful - *Xiao xin (sheow shin)* 小心

Wait a minute - *Deng yi deng (dung yee dung)* 等一等

A very good baby - *Hen hao de bao bao*

    (hun how de bow bow) 很好的宝宝

Goodbye - *Zai jian (tsai jian)* 再见

Dad - *Ba ba (ba ba)* 爸爸

Two tigers - *Liang zhi lao hu*

    (liang jer lao who) 两只老虎

Good morning - *Zao an (zao an)* 早安

Very pretty - *Hen piao liang (hun peow liang)* 很漂亮

Go home - *Hui jia (hway jia)* 回家

Five kwai - *Wu kuai qian (wu kwai chian)* 五块钱

CONTENTS

CONTENTS

Chapter One

News!

As soon as Mom walks in the door, the phone rings. "Yes, I see, how wonderful!" Mom holds the phone with her shoulder so she can put Kaylee into her booster seat and pour Ken a glass of milk. "We are very happy. Congratulations!" She sounds distracted and then hands the phone to me.

"Great news!" Ms. Sylvester's voice is loud. "We've finally been approved!"

"Finally" is right. Last February, Ms. Sylvester and her husband came to our house to talk about adopting a baby from China. Everyone was so excited, and Mom said that maybe she and I could go with them to help. The Sylvesters even offered to pay for my ticket. But the process took forever.

Ms. Sylvester is talking fast. "The baby's name is Jing and we are hoping that you and your mom can go to China with us to pick her up over winter break."

"I hope so," I tell her. Silently, I think that Jing Sylvester sounds funny, but then I realize that it's no different from *Anna* with *Wang*.

"How do you like middle school so far?" Ms. Sylvester asks.

I'm not sure what to say. The cafeteria is really crowded, and now that Laura is going to Our Lady of Angels, Camille is my only friend. But I can't explain all that on the phone. "Fine," I mumble.

"Okay, Anna, I'm sure I'll see you soon."

I hang up the phone. February, March, April, May, June, July, August, September. I've been waiting to hear this news for eight months, but now that it's real, my stomach feels tight. What will it be like to visit a place where almost everyone is Chinese? And what if

I hate the food? Mom says Chinese food in America is completely different from Chinese food in China.

Ken takes his glass to the sink and runs out the door. Kaylee is eating Cheerios by the handful. "Can we go with the Sylvesters to get their baby?" I ask.

"The tickets are very expensive now," Mom says. She pours milk into a sippy cup for Kaylee. "I know that the Sylvesters said they will pay for you, but we still have to buy my ticket."

"Maybe I can earn some money by babysitting," I say.

Mom looks out the window above the kitchen sink. "First we can go to Beijing to help the Sylvesters and see Kaylee's orphanage, and from there we can go to Shanghai to visit my family." Mom's eyes have a faraway look. "But that would take much longer than two weeks. Even one month would be too short."

I really want my mother to come with me to China. That's been our plan all along. "How about three weeks?" I suggest.

Mom wipes Kaylee's face with a washcloth. "Just today two of the nurses on my floor asked for time off before the holidays. I am new. I cannot ask for so much vacation." Mom closes her eyes. "Maybe in a couple of years, we can plan a longer trip."

"So we can't go?"

Mom takes a deep breath. "This is not a good time for me, Anna."

I can't believe that the Sylvesters finally got approved and now Mom says we can't go! Who knows what could happen in a couple of years? By then I'll be in high school. "Can I go to China without you?"

As soon as the words are out of my mouth, I feel

unsure. How would it feel to go so far away without anyone in my family? I know Ms. Sylvester because she was my teacher for two years, but she's not like an aunt or someone I've known forever. And I've only met her husband once.

Mom fingers the buttons on her sweater. "You never stayed away from home before."

Mom is right. I only spent the night at Camille's once, and in the middle of the night I missed home so much that Camille's mother called Dad to come and pick me up. "This is different from a sleepover," I say.

Mom bends down to clean up the Cheerios that landed on the floor. "I don't know, Anna. You are only eleven years old. And two weeks is a long time." She takes Kaylee out of her seat and sets her on the floor. "But the decision is for you."

Kaylee runs over and hugs me around my legs. "Play with me," she says.

Two weeks would be a long time without Kaylee and Mom and Dad and Ken and our cat Maow Maow. But a couple of years is too long to wait.

"I want to go," I whisper.

Chapter Two

A Lucky Day

Dad drops me off at school on his way to work. I stand outside my homeroom and wait for Camille. Kids are coming in the front door, closing their umbrellas, and going to their lockers. There are lots of white kids and some African American kids, but I think Camille and I are the only two Asians in the whole sixth grade, maybe even in all of Fenwick Middle School.

As soon as Camille comes through the door, she waves. We sit together underneath the window and she takes a list out of her backpack. "My mom says I can't join more than three clubs at the very most." Camille has circled the ones she's interested in. "What about you?"

The hallway is getting really hot and noisy, and I can't imagine staying in the school building any longer than I have to. "I don't think I'll join anything for now." I tell Camille that the Sylvesters finally got approved to adopt their baby, but now my mom can't get off work, so I might go without her. "If I do end up going to China, I'll have to miss a couple of weeks of school."

"My parents would never let me do that," Camille says. "They won't let me miss a single tutoring session."

The bell rings and we head to class. The social studies teacher, Ms. Remick, has the schedule on the board.

"We will have a shortened period this morning," she explains, "to leave time for club shopping."

Our new unit is called "Who Am I?" Ms. Remick asks us to reflect for a minute on what makes us who we are.

Allison raises her hand. "Our parents and grandparents."

"I was born in China," Camille says. "And that makes me who I am."

I'm always surprised at the way Camille tells everyone she's Chinese. I usually wait, hoping nobody will ask if I'm Chinese or Japanese, or if I eat with chopsticks.

"My grandpa makes me who I am," Lamar says. "Next summer he's taking me on a fishing trip to Canada."

"My grandparents took us to Disney World," Amber says.

I never met either of my grandfathers because they died before I was born. When we went to China, I met my mom's mom and some of my aunts and uncles, but I was too little to remember very much. The only grandparent I know is my dad's mom, who lives in California.

Ms. Remick nods. "Who we are depends on many factors," she continues. "One of the things that influences each of us is the community we live in. So our first unit will be an oral history project."

Camille pokes me. "What's that?" She always panics when she's not completely sure what's going on, and then she misses the rest of the explanation.

"We will interview people in our communities," Ms. Remick says as she passes out a packet that describes our assignment. The project is due at the end of the semester.

Everybody starts talking at once. Lucy wants to interview her great-grandpa, and Camille says she might pick Teacher Zhao, from Chinese School. I could interview Ray, the crossing guard at North Fairmont Elementary, because he tells good stories, but I'd rather choose someone I don't know yet, like Kaylee's birth mother. But it would be impossible to interview someone that you don't know anything about and who you couldn't find no matter how hard you searched.

It's time to pack up and head over to the gym. "Hurry," Camille says, pulling me toward the door.

A sign on the wall of the gym reads FENWICK MIDDLE SCHOOL: ACTIVE. ENGAGED. SUCCESSFUL. Tables are set up in rows with the names of the clubs on cards. Students walk around in clumps of three or four, laughing and talking. Three girls dressed in identical skinny jeans and pink sweatshirts are huddled together. I hurry past, hoping they don't notice my baggy jeans.

Camille heads over to the track team, and I make my way toward a table with only two kids—a girl with curly hair and a short boy with glasses. The sign says COMMUNITY ACTION TEAM: MAKE A DIFFERENCE. I step closer. A laptop shows pictures of kids collecting trash in an empty lot.

"Want to join CAT?" the girl asks. "I'm Andee with two *e*'s, and this is Sam." Her face is wide and open, and her eyes look kind of Asian. She is wearing long earrings that move as she talks. I think they're cut out of Coke cans and I wonder if she made them herself. "We meet on Wednesdays."

"I don't know," I say. "I might be going to China." I wonder if the other members of CAT are seventh- and eighth-graders who already know each other.

"You can always miss a few meetings." Andee stops the computer slide show at a picture of a chubby girl with dark skin and small braids. "That's Sierra. I mentor her every Monday."

"What do you do together?"

"Sometimes I help her with her homework, but usually we just walk to Dairy Queen." Andee pushes one of her curls behind her ear. "I'm trying to get her to open up to me."

For a minute I wish Andee were mentoring me. Maybe then Fenwick would seem more friendly. I pick up the pen on the table and write my name, ANNA WANG, on the sign-up sheet.

Andee smiles and I see that her teeth are covered with braces. "We have the same initials. Anna Wang and Andee Wu," she says.

Our eyes meet. "Are you Chinese?"

"Half," she says.

I wonder if people will ask us if we're cousins like

they did when Camille first joined North Fairmount. Or will Andee's tight curls make us seem too different? I want to ask Andee if she speaks Chinese, but the gym is so noisy that it's impossible to have a conversation. "See you Wednesday," I say, moving toward the door.

On the way home on the bus, Camille is quiet.

"Did you sign up for track tryouts?" I ask.

She nods. "But I don't see how I can do anything at this school except study. Do you believe that packet Ms. Remick gave us? It's about twenty pages."

"Most of it is definitions and instructions."

Camille plays with the strap of her backpack, rolling and unrolling it. "Maybe I should have repeated fifth grade."

"I bet it'll get easier," I say. But I'm not sure if it really will for Camille. Sometimes when I explain directions to her, she has trouble following the steps. We're close to my stop, so I stand up and move toward the door. "I'll call you later."

Camille forces a smile. "My tutor leaves at five."

I get off the bus alone. Last year I walked home with Laura. We kicked sweet gum balls and caught leaves and talked the whole way down the hill. And if Laura was going to her dad's, I walked with Ken. But Ken is still at North Fairmount and Laura doesn't get home until four thirty, and then we both have homework. When she does come over, she talks about new friends I don't know.

Acorns crunch under my shoes. The air is warm and windy, as if fall is about to start but summer is still hanging on. I'm lucky that Camille goes to Fenwick with me. But lately it seems we're so different. The other day I told her that sometimes I lie in bed at night wishing I wasn't Chinese. *Really?* she said, pulling her eyebrows together. Her face looked hurt and I wished I could take back my words. *I can't imagine* not *being Chinese,* she said.

When I get to my house, I take the key out of my backpack and open the door. Mom and Dad are at work, Ken comes home half an hour later than me, and Kaylee stays at daycare until Mom or Dad can pick her up. I pour myself a glass of milk and add two big spoons of Nestlé Quik. Then I get a fortune cookie out of the big bag Grandma sent from San Francisco, crack it in half, and read the small, typed words: *Today is your lucky day.* After the sentence is the Chinese character that I think means "happiness."

幸福

Mom doesn't like fortune cookies. She says they don't even exist in China, and that it's impossible to predict the future. She cringes when we get fortunes like *You will be a millionaire.* Hard work is important for happiness, she says, not money or luck. *If you work hard, you can reach your goal,* she always says.

I know Mom is mostly right. If you don't study Spanish vocabulary, you won't pass the test no matter how much you wish for good luck. But then some people learn things faster than others, and that's luck. And some babies are born into families where their parents can take care of them and other babies are left on the steps of an office building like my sister. Isn't that luck too?

I fold the slip of paper with the fortune written on it and put it into my jeans pocket.

Chapter Three
CAT

Quizzes make the day go by fast. Pre-algebra is easy. The English test has picky multiple-choice grammar questions, but I can get most of them just by what sounds right. I glance at the clock. Two forty-five. Why did I ever sign up for CAT?

When the bell rings, I stop in front of room 203 and look inside. A teacher is at the desk, grading papers. Sam and Andee and one other girl are sitting on the floor.

Andee sees me. "Hi, Anna. This is Simone."

Simone scoots over to make a space for me. She has dark skin and her hair is braided in a spiral around

her head. She has a pencil sticking out from behind her ear.

"Saturday we're doing a cleanup in Over-the-Rhine," Sam says. "Can you come?"

I shake my head. "I have Chinese class." For some reason, I don't feel weird telling Sam and Andee and Simone that I'm learning Chinese.

"I wish I knew Chinese," Sam says. "The only thing I can say is *Ni hao*."

"*Wo hen hao*," I say in response.

"*Wo hen hao*," he tries to repeat. "I think if I could pick a language to learn, it would be Chinese."

"You could come to Saturday Chinese School," I say. "They have a beginner's level."

Sam shakes his head. "My family's Jewish, so I have to go to Hebrew school at least until I'm sixteen. Then I can decide if I want to quit or start another language."

I can't imagine learning any other language besides Chinese. Whenever Mom's talking to her friends, I wish I could understand everything.

Sam is organizing the transportation to the cleanup. Andee and Simone and I start brainstorming about places where we can volunteer, like the Senior Center downtown, the Boys and Girls Club, and the Main Library Homework Central. Simone writes everything down on a legal pad and we try to make a schedule for the activities.

When I glance at the clock, it's already almost three thirty. "I'd better go. My dad's picking me up."

"Thanks for coming." Andee stands up. "And tell your friends to come to our next meeting, Wednesday at lunchtime."

I nod even though I don't really have any friends

at this school except Camille, and she isn't allowed to join another club. I walk past the gym. Camille is in her shorts, taller than everyone else, standing in a long line of girls who are trying to make it onto the track team. I bet her legs are shaking. I wish I had the lucky-day fortune to give to her, but it's at home in my jeans pocket.

After dinner, I sit down at the computer and type "Lucky Family Orphanage, Beijing" into Google like I've done many times before. It always comes up with "Site Under Construction." But suddenly there's a picture of a drab-looking two-story building with Chinese characters on the front.

"It's here!" I say.

I pick Kaylee up and hold her on my lap. "You used to live there."

"No," Kaylee says.

Mom looks at the computer screen. "That must be it."

I zoom in on the front of the building and we can see a lady standing in the doorway. There is nothing else on the site yet except the navigation bars, which don't work. "Why weren't you allowed to go to the orphanage when you adopted Kaylee?" I ask again.

"The adoption agency said they always do it that way. Probably they don't want *wai guo ren* going there and telling them all the things wrong with the orphanage."

"Even if you're a foreigner, I still think you should have the right to see where your baby lived," I say. "That's where you lived when you were a baby," I tell Kaylee.

"No," Kaylee says again. She puts her thumb into her mouth and looks as if she's about to cry.

I rest my chin on the top of her head. "Now you live here. With Mom and Dad and Ken and me and Maow Maow."

"And Kaylee," she says, turning so that she can rub her face in my sweater.

Mom goes to the stove to stir the rice porridge that I love. "What did your family in China think when you and Dad decided to adopt a baby?" I ask.

"My sister said we already had two children, a boy

and a girl, so why? In China you can only have one child. Two is already too many. But I told her that I miss a big family." Mom adds water to the porridge. "And there is another thing. I think of the families who have to give up their second baby. Then my sister understood."

"What about Grandma Nai Nai?"

Mom smiles. "She knows a big family is good. She had eleven brothers and sisters."

"Do all the families in China now really only have one kid?"

"Not all. But most. If you have more children, you have to give them up for adoption or you have to pay a fine. And many people do not have this money."

"I think that's mean."

"There are too many people in China. They have to solve this problem."

It's strange to think that if Mom and Dad had stayed in China, I probably wouldn't have Ken for a brother or Kaylee for a sister. I also wouldn't be living in this house and talking English and staring at this computer screen. I wonder if my parents ever considered living in China. I know they met when Dad was visiting his grandparents. Mom was working as a secretary in the hotel where he was staying. But I don't know much else.

Kaylee is leaning her head against my chest and her eyes are starting to close. She opens them, looks at me, then closes them again. She looks so perfect when she's falling asleep, with her black hair all messed up and her thumb in her mouth. I wonder who held Kaylee when she was a little baby. Or did she fall asleep alone in a crib?

"Are you sure you can't take time off to go to China?" I ask.

Mom looks down. "In two or three years, Anna." She picks Kaylee gently off my lap, lays her down on the sofa, and puts my jacket over her like a blanket. Then we sit together in the armchair like we used to when I was little. "This time you will go to China with the Sylvesters. And next time we will go together to see my family."

"Are they all still in Shanghai?"

"One brother is in Singapore. I am the only one in America."

"Do you miss them?"

"Every day," Mom whispers.

I look at Mom's face to see if being so far from her family makes her sad. "Sometimes do you wish you had stayed?" I ask.

Mom pulls me close. "No reason to look back and wish this or wish that. I do not wish anything. I have my family."

Chapter Four

I Am From

The English teacher, Mrs. Smith, talks in a monotone. My stomach growls and I consider trying to sneak a bite of my bagel, but my seat is too close to her desk.

MEAL, Mrs. Smith writes in big letters. "Does anyone know what this stands for besides a time when we eat?"

Robert raises his hand. "I'm hungry."

Mrs. Smith doesn't give him a detention even though his comment is obviously disrespectful. I

THE YEAR OF THE FORTUNE COOKIE

feel sorry for Mrs. Smith, but I don't know what MEAL stands for and neither does anyone else. Finally she tells us. M is for main idea, E is for evidence, A is for analysis, and L is the last sentence. In other words, MEAL is the way we are supposed to write a paragraph.

Then she says she has been working with Ms. Remick on the "Who Am I" unit, and we will start by analyzing poetry. She passes out a piece of paper with a poem written on it.

"Would anyone like to read this poem out loud?" she asks.

Nobody volunteers, so she reads it to us. "'Where I'm From' by George Ella Lyons . . .

"I am from clothespins,
from Clorox and carbon-tetrachloride.
I am from the dirt under the back porch.
(Black, glistening,
it tasted like beets.)
I am from the forsythia bush
the Dutch elm

whose long-gone limbs I remember
as if they were my own.
I'm from fudge and eyeglasses,
      from Imogene and Alafair."

A few students laugh because they think Imogene
and Alafair are funny names. Mrs. Smith stops reading to quiet the class, giving me time to think.

I'm from honeysuckle bushes in our backyard and
paper airplanes and Mom's Chinese hamburgers. I
wish I had one right now. Mrs. Smith starts again:

"Under my bed was a dress box
spilling old pictures,
a sift of lost faces
to drift beneath my dreams.
I am from those moments—
snapped before I budded—
leaf-fall from the family tree."

When Mrs. Smith is done, people start to gather up
their things, but she tells us that the bell has not rung

yet and she wants us to begin to analyze the poem using MEAL.

I like the poem, but I don't know what to write. Ms. Sylvester used to let us just write what we thought of. I would have said that I like this poem because I used to play under the back porch, so I know what the writer means by the taste of dirt. But that certainly isn't the main idea.

Camille pokes me with her elbow. "I don't get it. What's MEAL?"

Mrs. Smith tells her to stop talking.

Finally I start writing:

> The main idea of this poem is that lots of things make us who we are. The part I like best is "Under my bed was a dress box spilling old pictures, a sift of lost faces to drift beneath my dreams." I like how the box was so full that the pictures spilled out, and then she dreamed about them because those faces were part of who she was. If I was writing a poem about who I am, I

would include all the pictures on my bulletin
board of my family, but we only have a few
pictures from before I was born."

I reread the poem. I wish we had more old pictures.
Once, Laura showed me her family photo album that
had pictures from the 1800s. She said they traced
their family's roots all the way back to the *Mayflower*.
I wonder if there might be some way that I could find
out more about my ancestors. Maybe when Mom and
I go to China together, we can try.

I doodle on the paper. Then I write,

I am from bulletin boards
with photos
of my family,
Mom and Dad in Shanghai
before I was born,
and my sister in China
the day she left.
Does she remember?
I am from a kitchen

that smells like anise and garlic
and Grandma's seaweed soup.
I am from a slip of paper
with my fortune:
Today is your lucky day.

When the bell rings, I realize that I wrote the poem on the same paper as the MEAL paragraph, but it's too late to copy it over. We put our papers in the teacher's basket, and it's time for lunch.

Chapter Five
Gathering Signatures

Dad takes me to school early on Monday because if I'm going to get an approved absence to go to China, I have to get a form signed by all my teachers and the principal and then submit it to the Board of Education for processing, which can take several weeks. The Sylvesters have not bought our plane tickets yet, but they said we will probably be gone from December 12 to 24. The semester ends on December 22, so I'll have to miss eleven days of school.

First I go to Ms. Remick's classroom. "Anna, so nice to see you bright and early."

I take out the form and my words tumble over each

other as I tell her about going to China with my teacher from last year, who is going to adopt a baby.

"My, aren't you lucky." She takes off her glasses. "I have always dreamed of visiting the Great Wall." She signs the form and hands it to me. "Please take a lot of pictures to show us."

"Thank you," I say, hurrying out of the room.

The math teacher looks at my quiz grades, which are all above 90, and then signs the form. The life science and Spanish teachers ask me a few questions about the trip and then sign. The only one left is Mrs. Smith. I hesitate for a minute before knocking on her door.

"Come in," she says, barely looking up.

I hand her the paper. "So, you are planning to miss almost two weeks of school?" she asks after a minute.

I nod.

"Didn't you say that your sister was adopted from China?"

I blush, remembering the poem that I scrawled on

the bottom of my paper. "Yes. Now I'm planning to go with my teacher from last year."

"Two weeks is a lot to miss unless there is a very good reason." She turns back to her computer. "I'll give it some thought."

I walk quickly out of the room.

"She didn't sign it," I tell Camille at lunch.

"Did you explain about how you're going to help the Sylvesters?"

I shake my head. "She always seems too busy to

talk. Plus, it's not really true. I mean, the Sylvesters could adopt their baby without me."

Camille tilts her head. "They don't know much Chinese, plus they probably don't know anything about babies since they never had one. You're so good with your sister. Mrs. Smith doesn't know that." She picks up her sandwich. "You're good at writing, too. Maybe you should write a paragraph about all the reasons you want to go."

I think for a minute. "I'm not even sure what they are."

"My tutor told me that sometimes you get ideas when you're actually writing them down."

It's funny how when I talk to Camille, I feel so much better. I wonder if I do that for her, too.

"I'm still not sure who I should do for my oral history project," she says.

"I thought you wanted to interview Teacher Zhao."

"I think my grandpa would be better. But the problem is, he doesn't live here, so he's not really part of the community."

I chew my apple slowly. Camille's grandpa comes to visit every summer. She told me how he helped her learn to sound out words by reading her poems and songs that she loved. Just because he lives in Oklahoma doesn't mean he isn't part of her community. "He is, if you make the community bigger," I say.

Camille smiles. "I never thought of that. Like the whole United States?"

"Or even the whole world."

Really, couldn't you interview anyone in the world? The definition of *community* in our packet said "a group of people whose lives are connected." But isn't everyone connected to everyone else? You start with people who are close to you and it goes out like a spider's web. I am connected to my parents and they are connected to their parents and grandparents. When I go to China, if I get to go, my life could be connected to someone I meet there. Maybe I could interview the people who took care of Kaylee or the man who brought her to my parents at the hotel when they adopted her. I could explain to Mrs. Smith that going

to China will be part of my oral history project. How
could she say no to that?

As soon as I get home, I start my paragraph:

Almost one year ago, my teacher from fourth
and fifth grades, Ms. Sylvester, told me that
they wanted to adopt a baby from China.
My mom and I thought we should go with
them because the Sylvesters don't speak
much Chinese and they don't know a lot
about babies either. But it turns out my
mom can't go. I am hoping I can still go
with them for many reasons. My little sister
Kaylee was adopted from the same orphanage
near Beijing, and I want to go and see where
she came from. This is important because

I get stuck. Because what? I probably won't even be
able to go to the orphanage. Then what will I do for
my oral history project? I turn the paper over and start
again.

One day a little baby was wrapped in a blanket and left on the steps of an office building. Somebody found her and took her to an orphanage, where they called her Bao Bao. Now she is a three-year-old little girl named Kaylee, who is my sister.

It's hard to explain why it is so important to me to go to China. Part of it is that I want to see where Kaylee is from. I want to talk to the people who work at the orphanage to see if they remember anything about my sister when they first got her. I want to meet the man who brought her to my parents. Maybe there is nothing more to find out, but I will do my best to learn what I can. I hope I can interview someone at the orphanage for my oral history project.

I also want to help my teacher, because a new baby is really hard. My sister cried a lot, and I sang her lots of Chinese songs to calm her down. I can do the same thing with my teacher's new baby.

The other thing is that I am Chinese, so I think it's important to see what China is like.

I reread that line. It seems unnecessary to write that I am Chinese when of course Mrs. Smith knows that from my face and my name. But it also seems like the most important line in my essay.

At the end, I add a note: I know we are supposed to use MEAL, but I don't have any evidence about the orphanage yet.

Chapter Six

Fortune Cookies

As soon as I get to school, I go to Mrs. Smith's room to deliver my essay. She's not there, so I put my paper on her chair and hurry to social studies.

I'm really starting to look forward to Ms. Remick's class. I like the way she connects everything. We're talking about slavery now and our responsibility to keep stories alive and how those stories are part of who we are.

"What if nobody writes down stories of the past?" she asks.

Lucy raises her hand. "Then we forget them."

Ms. Remick nods. "And what if we only read one story about what happened?"

I raise my hand. "Then we don't know if it's true."

Ms. Remick nods again. "How do you think we can learn the stories of people who were enslaved?" she asks.

"Did some slaves write down what happened to them?" Simon asks.

"Some. But it was very difficult for enslaved people to learn to read and write. In fact, it was considered a crime for which they could be punished. Any other ideas?"

Nobody knows.

"Sometimes we can use documents or old pictures." Ms. Remick shows us a record of slave sales. *Strong back, good teeth, 500 dollars*, it says. The words turn my stomach. Then she shows us pictures of a slave auction. There is an auctioneer measuring a man who is being sold. He is standing on a step called an auction block. I see my classmates shifting their feet under their desks. I learned about slavery in second, third, and fourth grades, but I never really thought of a person being sold.

Ms. Remick says she knows it is hard to look at some of the pictures, but it is all part of learning what happened in the past. By piecing together a lot of things, you can start to get a whole picture. "It's kind of like being a detective," she says. "You have to make some guesses and then see if they're true."

"We did that last year when we did our science fair projects," Camille says.

"Good connection," Ms. Remick says. "I never thought about how similar studying history is to studying science."

"In fourth grade, we made timelines of our lives," Simon says. "That was kind of like piecing a puzzle together too, because you can't remember when you were really little."

"Another wonderful connection." Ms. Remick seems so genuinely pleased with our ideas.

"My grandpa made me a timeline of his life," Camille says. "To show me when my dad was born, and my aunts and uncles, too. It was so long, it went across our whole living room."

I wish my mother would make me a timeline of her life. When Grandma comes from California, she tells me about Dad when he was little. But Mom doesn't talk much about her life in China. We have one picture of her with her sisters and brothers in a park in Shanghai, and another of her parents on their wedding day. Since I was three when we visited her family in Shanghai, I can hardly remember anything. Sometimes I want to ask Mom more, but it seems to make her sad.

When I get to the lunchtime CAT meeting, Andee is the only one there. She says the teacher at Our Lady of Angels wants to see if that school and ours can do some projects together. "She suggested fundraising for a cause, but it's sort of hard to just raise money for something we don't know that much about and then send a check. I mean, we raised three hundred dollars for the orphanage in Africa, but we never really felt connected."

"I feel connected to an orphanage," I hear myself saying. "Sort of." And then, all of a sudden, I'm telling her about my sister. "When my parents went to China to adopt her, they couldn't actually go to the orphanage. I'm hoping I can visit it this winter."

Andee is listening hard. "Do you know anything about the orphanage, like what they might need?"

I shake my head. "The only thing I know is that it's called the Lucky Family Orphanage."

Andee smiles, and I see that she has fluorescent green rubber bands on her braces that match her earrings. "I wonder if they named it that because the orphans form a lucky family or because whoever adopts them is a lucky family."

I think about that for a minute. I hope Kaylee feels lucky that Mom and Dad adopted her. But I hope she also feels lucky that someone found her and took her to the orphanage where people took care of her. "Maybe a little of both."

"Either way, we could have a Lucky Family Bake Sale to raise money," Andee says.

Thinking about luck gives me an idea. "We could bake fortune cookies."

Andee is quiet for a minute. Maybe she thinks fortune cookies are a dumb idea. "I wonder," she says, "if two Asian kids sell fortune cookies, do you think people will think . . . I mean, it's such a stereotype."

I know what Mom would say. *Don't worry about what people think or who is what race.* But Andee is right. Suddenly there's something I have to know. "Do people ask you what you are?"

Andee plays with her earrings. "All the time. Mostly they ask me where I'm from, or when I'm with my mom, they ask me if I'm adopted." She looks up. "What about you?"

"In elementary school, a couple of the boys pulled the corners of their eyes at me and chanted *Anna Wang, Ching Chung Chang.*" I don't think I've ever told this to anyone.

Andee looks sad. "I didn't really hear stuff like that."

"Did your teachers mix you up with other Asian girls?" I ask, thinking of how people thought Camille was my cousin.

Andee nods. "All the time."

"Maybe we should just bake regular chocolate chip cookies," I say.

"The thing is, fortune cookies would be more fun to make, and I think people would buy them, which is the whole point of a bake sale. Plus it won't be just us selling them. It'll be Sam and Simone and everyone in CAT." She is talking faster now.

"My mom said that fortune cookies don't even exist in China."

Andee hands me a slice of apple. "That's funny. I just assumed they were invented there."

"My mom never saw them until she got to the U.S."

"Let's go for it. The Lucky Family Fortune Cookie Bake Sale. I'll contact the teacher at Our Lady of Angels, and we can bake the cookies at my house."

"One of my best friends from elementary school goes to that school."

"Do you think she's in their community service group?"

"I'm not sure. Now that we go to different schools, I don't see her that often."

I hear a knock on the door, and Mrs. Smith is there. "Anna, I enjoyed your essay. It is much improved. But you could make it stronger with a few changes." She

gives me the paper, which has red marks and comments all over the margins. "I'd like to see a revision."

"Thank you," I mumble.

Then she hands me the permission form, and in red pen, she signed her name!

When I get home, I read the comments. *Be more specific. Explain exactly what you mean.* At the end of the essay, Mrs. Smith has written a note:

Dear Anna, thank you for explaining to me why it is so important for you to go to China. Now I understand that this is a chance for you not only to help your teacher and to learn more about your sister but also to learn more about yourself.

Your essay would be stronger if the ideas were in a logical order. Maybe you should consider putting the last sentence first since it seems like the main idea. I understand that you cannot find evidence for everything, but points still need to be supported.

Yours,
Mrs. Smith

I take out a clean sheet of paper and write:

Main Idea

I am Chinese, so it is important for me to see what China is like. In America the first thing people notice about me is that I am Asian, but in China, that will be different.

Being Chinese is important for my life and for my family. My dad was born in the U.S. but my mom was born in China. Even though I can't visit her family on this trip because I am going to Beijing and they are in Shanghai, this is still one reason I want to go to China. It is important to learn about the country where my mother grew up.

The other reason is that my sister was

adopted from China. I hope I can visit her orphanage, but even if I can't I will find out more about China. That is also part of her story, and mine, too. She was born in China and I wasn't, but we are both Chinese. And the best way to learn about China is to go there.

Once I started with the main idea, everything fell into place.

Chapter Seven
Baking Day

$\mathcal{I}$t takes us about half an hour to get to Andee's house. Mom keeps saying we must be lost, but we're following the directions that Andee sent. Take I-71, get off at Indian Hill, then wind along Indian Hill Road for a long time, past yards so big you can't see the houses and Horse Crossing signs. Finally we see her house number and turn down a long driveway. I can't believe Andee goes to Fenwick Middle School from way out here.

She hugs me as soon as she opens the door. "I'm so glad you came early."

I look around the kitchen, which is bigger than our

living room. There are two computers and two ovens, and the refrigerator is three big drawers. "This kitchen is huge." After the words are out of my mouth, I wish I hadn't said them.

Andee blushes. "I know. Sometimes I feel . . . kind of embarrassed about this house."

"It's very nice." I look out the front window. "Isn't there a school closer than Fenwick?"

"I was kind of miserable in my old school." She pulls her hair back into a ponytail. "It's hard to explain. I mean, everyone thought my ideas were really strange. So my parents finally said I could transfer to Fenwick."

"I didn't know you could just transfer to another school if you don't live there."

"We have to pay tuition," Andee says. "But it's worth it." She goes over to the counter where there are grocery bags full of the ingredients. "We'd better get organized." She takes out cutting boards, mixing bowls, whisks, a mixer, spatulas, and spoons.

"Are your parents home?" I ask.

"My mom's upstairs." She sits down at one of the computers in the kitchen and pulls up the fortune cookie recipe.

When the doorbell rings, I open the door and it's Laura!

"Hey, Anna, I didn't know you'd be here!"

"And I didn't know you'd be here." Laura smiles, and suddenly I realize how much I've missed her. I introduce her to Andee, and soon there are six more kids, three from Our Lady of Angels and Simone and Sam and a girl named Hideat. Sam sits down at the computer and everyone starts shouting out ideas for fortunes:

"This is your lucky day, because you donated to the Lucky Family Orphanage."

"Thank you from the Lucky Family Orphanage."

"You may not win the lottery, but you will help a baby at the Lucky Family Orphanage," Laura says.

Sam is typing as

fast as he can. Then we print out the fortunes and cut them into strips.

We decide to triple the recipe. To make the batter, we have to first separate the egg yolks from the whites and beat up the whites with the mixer. Then we melt the butter and mix all the ingredients together. We put it by spoonfuls onto the greased cookie sheets, and slide them into the oven. "It says to bake them for five to eight minutes," Andee says,

setting the oven timer to six. Then she turns the kitchen computer so everyone can see it, and we watch a YouTube video about how to fold the fortune cookies.

"If we're too slow, they'll break," I say.

"And if we're too fast, we'll burn our hands," Laura says.

❋ ❋ ❋

As soon as the timer rings, we get to work in small groups. The cookies are thin like flat pancakes. Sam takes one off the sheet, Laura puts the fortune on it, I fold the cookie in half and  bend the edges up, and Hideat sets it on a rack to cool. When we're done, there are ninety-two cookies on the racks.

"If we sell them for two dollars each, that's almost two hundred dollars," Hideat says.

When the cookies are cool, we pack them carefully in two boxes, one to take to Our Lady of Angels and one for Fenwick. We wash the dishes and clean off the counters, and Andee's parents never come down. It would be strange to have a house so big that you didn't see or hear anyone else for hours.

When everyone is gone, I follow Andee upstairs, where she introduces me to her mom, who is sitting at a desk in a kind of upstairs living room. "Andee told me about you," her mom says. She has a wide smile just like her daughter, and very curly hair. "I heard you have a trip to China coming up."

"I'll be going in December." Suddenly my trip sounds really soon.

Andee shows me her room, which is big with white walls and framed posters all around. She has a bathroom all to herself, and a little alcove that she calls the Art Spot. On the table are a few acorns and buckeyes and earring hooks.

"My brother and sister always get into my art and sewing stuff," I tell her.

"You're lucky to have siblings," Andee says.

"Sometimes."

"My parents were kind of old when they had me. Plus they have to travel a lot for work."

We look at pictures she has framed on her desk, of her parents with her when she was a baby. "You were so cute," I say. "You look like both your parents."

"I have my mom's hair," she says.

"And your dad's eyes," I say.

When Dad comes to pick me up, I can't believe the afternoon is already over.

Chapter Eight

Baby Gifts

After school I leave my revised essay on Mrs. Smith's desk and head over to the gym. Andee already has everything set up, including a big sign that says SUPPORT THE LUCKY FAMILY ORPHANAGE. Under that she has written the Chinese characters for "thank you," *xie xie*.

"Did your dad show you how to write the characters?" I ask.

"Actually, my mom knows Chinese better than my dad, so she helped me."

Camille stops by. "I know I'm not in CAT, but can I help?"

Andee gives her some tape and asks her to put up a

few signs in the hallway. A kid comes up to the table with two dollars. I hand him a cookie. He cracks it in half, takes out the fortune, and reads it. "Where's the Lucky Family Orphanage?" he asks.

"China."

He shows it to his friend. Soon kids start crowding around the table with two dollars in their hands. Mrs. Smith asks for five cookies, four for her nieces and one for herself. I put the cookies in a baggie and hand them to her. She gives me a twenty-dollar bill but she doesn't want change. "It's a donation," she says.

By four o'clock we've sold out, and we have more than two hundred dollars in the coffee can.

When I get home, Mom is talking to Ms. Sylvester on the phone. They bought our tickets for December 11, returning December 24. I stare at the calendar by the phone. I'll be gone for thirteen days, just before Christmas. That means I won't be home to decorate our tree or make Christmas presents with Grandma or bake sugar cookies with Laura like we usually do.

Mom is explaining to Ms. Sylvester that it is important in China to give gifts to everyone, so she should take lots of things for the orphanage workers and the people who are organizing the adoption trip. Mom thinks small bottles of lotion and pretty soaps would be nice.

I look out the window. It is only November, but the cold came early this year and the trees are bare. The sky is white and there are snow flurries blowing around. I wonder how it looks in Beijing. It's cold there in winter, just like here. Snowflakes must look the same all over the world.

Gifts for everyone, Mom says. But what about gifts for the babies? I know I'm taking money for the orphanage, but that's not the same as a gift. Mom thinks that there were about fifty baby girls at the orphanage when they adopted Kaylee. What can I give to fifty babies? I see a ball of red yarn in the basket where we keep the newspapers. I could knit a few baby hats, but there's no way I could make so many.

I call Andee. "Do you know how to knit?"

"Yup. Why?"

I tell her about my hat idea.

"CAT can help," she says. "We can teach everybody how to knit." That's how Andee is. She takes my ideas and figures out how to make them work. "There's this place near here called the Yarn Basket. I'll ask them if they can donate yarn."

"My mom has lots of knitting needles."

"Hey, if my mom will bring me, can I come over to your house? We could plan this knitting project."

I look around our living room. Dad's accounting books and Mom's nursing journals are in a mess on the coffee table. Kaylee's toys are all over the floor. "Sure," I say. "Come on over."

I find Mom's knitting needles in the basket and cast on forty stitches. By the time Andee arrives, I've knitted three rows.

"This is my family," I say after she comes in and I hang up her jacket.

Mom is standing at the stove. "It's nice to meet you," she says, smiling at Andee.

Andee sits next to me on the sofa and starts knitting really fast. "I went through an obsessive knitting phase in sixth grade," she explains.

Kaylee comes over. "Mine," she says.

"Not for you," I say. "It's a baby hat."

"Mine," Kaylee repeats, trying to take my knitting.

I pry her fingers off the yarn and she screams as if I'm killing her. Finally she gets her mouse and glares at us from the beanbag chair.

"Your house is so . . . lively," Andee says. "I love it."

"You mean crazy," I say. "Let's go upstairs."

We sit on the floor of my room, knitting baby hats together.

After a while, we go down to the kitchen to have a snack. I know Andee likes apples, so I cut one up for the two of us. Then I take out two fortune cookies.

"I've only had these at restaurants," Andee says.

"My grandma in California keeps us supplied." I crack mine open. *Do not fear what you do not know,* it says.

"Isn't everyone afraid of things they don't know?" Andee asks.

I put the cookie in my mouth. "Sometimes these fortunes don't make much sense." Andee takes the slip of paper out of her cookie. *Life is too short to waste time.*

"We'd better get knitting," I say.

✳ ✳ ✳

It's hard to believe that
two hours have gone
by when Andee's mom
calls to say that she is in
front of the house to pick
Andee up.

"Thanks for having me," she says. "I had a great time."

I look at our hats. "Two down, forty-eight to go."

"Wednesday at noon we'll have knitting lessons."

"I'll make a flyer," I say.

We go downstairs and I walk Andee out to the car the way Mom does when her friends come over.

It's after ten but I still can't sleep. First I'm hot, then I'm cold, then Maow Maow curls up on my neck. My stomach churns every time I think of getting on an airplane with the Sylvesters. I wish Camille or Andee or Laura could go with me. What if I can't even go to the orphanage? What will I do with the money from our bake sale, and fifty baby hats?

❄ ❄ ❄

After school, I make the flyer:

> Got Yarn?
> Knit baby hats, for an orphanage.
> No experience necessary.
> Come to CAT Wed at noon.
> Room 203

There are seven people at our lunchtime CAT meeting, and we give everyone a short knitting lesson.

Sam tries to cast on the stitches, but the yarn is too limp in his hands. "This is harder than baking fortune cookies," he says.

I show him how to hold the yarn tighter, and after a while he starts to get the hang of it.

Mrs. Smith shows up with ten small, very evenly knitted hats. "I saw the flyers and thought I'd better get busy. I should be able to make a few more by the end of the week. I'll get my nieces going too." As usual, she seems in a hurry to leave.

When she's gone, Simone says, "I know most kids don't like Mrs. Smith very much, but I think she's just really shy."

"That's what I think," Hideat says. "Sometimes she seems kind of unfriendly, the way she's always rushing, but once you get to know her, she's nice."

Sam holds up his hat, which is three rows long. "I think I'm getting it." He turns to me. "Hey, when you go to China, can you take a picture of one of the babies with this hat on?"

I nod. "I'll try to remember."

Hideat asks me if I was born in China. Usually when people ask me that, I feel embarrassed, as if someone with a Chinese face could not possibly be born in Cincinnati. But for some reason, this time the question doesn't bother me. I shake my head. "Cincinnati University Hospital."

"I was born in Eritrea," she says. "My family came here when I was a baby."

I am not sure where Eritrea is or what language is spoken there, but I ask, "Do you speak Eritrean?"

She smiles. "Actually, the language is called Tigrinya. I can understand it, but I don't speak it very well."

Right before the bell rings, Andee hands me a blue envelope with my name on the front. "I made something for your trip," she says. "You can open it when you get to China."

I put the envelope into my notebook, and Andee, Hideat, and I walk out of the room together.

Chapter Nine

Packing

$\mathcal{I}$ make a packing list:

Two sweaters
My warmest corduroy pants
2 pairs of jeans
4-5 shirts
Long underwear
Pajamas
Underwear and socks (fourteen pairs of each)
Extra pair of shoes

I assemble everything on my bed and try to fit it into my suitcase. I roll up all the little knitted hats and stuff them around the edges and inside my extra pair of shoes, even though I probably won't be able to visit Kaylee's orphanage. I wrote a letter to the government agency that helped us get my sister, but they didn't write back. I can't send an email to the orphanage because there is nothing on the website except the picture of the building. Maybe the Lucky Family Orphanage doesn't even exist anymore. So then why am I going? Maybe I should have waited until Mom could go with me and we could visit her family.

It's too late to change my mind now. I put three books in my backpack: *Homesick* from Ms. Remick, *Chains* from Laura, and *The Call of the Wild* from Mom and Dad. I put the blue envelope from Andee in the inside pocket with our camera. Ms. Sylvester will keep my passport and the fortune cookie money, which Mom changed into Chinese currency at the bank.

On a piece of paper I write Laura's, Camille's, and Andee's addresses so I can send them postcards. Who else? Maybe Ms. Remick, Mrs. Smith, and of course

Ken and Kaylee and Mom and Dad, and Grandma. I fold the paper and put it into the backpack.

Kaylee sees one of the little hats on the bed. "Mine," she says.

"I already told you, these are for babies, remember? The babies in China." I pull Kaylee to my lap. "You can draw a picture for the babies."

She takes a marker and draws something that she says is our house. Then she tries to make circles for Mom and Dad and me and Ken and herself, but it just looks like scribbling. She hands the marker to me and says "Kaylee," so I write her name on the bottom.

I put the drawing into my backpack. Then I go downstairs, look through the pictures in our computer file, and pick out the best ones of our family. In my favorite one, Mom and Dad are laughing in the background while Kaylee is glaring at Maow Maow and holding her sock mouse. I pick another where I am pushing Ken on a swing at the playground. Then there's one with Ken giving Kaylee a piggyback ride. The last one is Kaylee "reading" to Grandma. I print the pictures on glossy photo paper, cut them apart, and put them into a small album I've had in my desk drawer forever. When all the photos are neatly arranged, I show them to Kaylee.

"Again," she says, even after we've looked through the album three times.

The doorbell rings, and there are Camille and her mom. "I have something for you," Camille says. She hands me a small package wrapped in red paper. "For your trip."

"Should I open it now or on the plane?"

Camille considers. "Now."

I unwrap it, and inside is a journal full of blank white paper. "Perfect!" I say, running my hand over the cover, which is solid green with the word JOURNAL printed in small black letters.

"Write down what happens—so you don't forget," Camille says.

"Thank you so, so much." I hug Camille.

We go up to my room and I show her my suitcase. "It looks like it's stuffed full of hats." She holds up a yellow one.

"I wish you were coming with me to China," I say, feeling a lump grow in my throat.

Camille looks at me. "I haven't been back since we left. Sometimes when I can't sleep I try to remember living in China and I can't. Then I try to think in Chinese, and I can't do that either."

"I can't even *imagine* thinking in Chinese," I say. I roll up the yellow hat and stuff it into the corner of the suitcase. Even when I swallow hard, the lump in my throat is still there. "I wish I could stay home."

"Two weeks isn't that long." Camille touches the journal. "I'll keep a diary too, and then we can swap."

Camille always knows just what to say.

Chapter Ten
The Trip

At the airport, Kaylee doesn't want to hug me, and when I try to kiss her cheek, she turns away. Ken is in a hurry to get back home so he can open the new Lego kit Grandma sent him.

Dad puts his arm around my shoulders. "Make sure to stay with the Sylvesters so you don't get lost."

When I turn to hug Mom, there are tears in her eyes.

"We'll take good care of her," Mr. Sylvester says, looking at me.

"And she'll take good care of us," Ms. Sylvester adds.

I try to swallow so I can say goodbye, but the words are stuck in my throat. Then it's time to give the lady our tickets and walk down the jetway.

The plane is full, and about half of the people are Chinese. I hear words that I understand, like *lai lai,* "come here," and *mei wen ti,* "no problem," but there is a lot of background noise and most people are talking too fast.

Six couples are going to China together to adopt their baby girls, but there are no other kids in the group except me. The Sylvesters and I have three seats in a row, and mine is the one by the window.

"Would you like a snack?" Mr. Sylvester asks, handing me a bag of trail mix.

I thank him, but the plane has not even taken off and my stomach is already churning.

"Keep it for later," he says.

A lady in the seat behind us taps me on the shoulder. "Are you going to see the place where you were adopted?" she asks.

"I'm not adopted," I say quickly. I've never been asked that before, and if I were adopted, I probably would not want to talk about it with a stranger.

The lady looks confused. "I'm sorry. I assumed you were going to see your first home."

"I'm going with my teacher and her husband. They're adopting a baby," I explain.

"Oh, how nice."

I lean back in my seat. What if I really were the Sylvesters' adopted daughter? Ms. Sylvester's hair is fine and curly, and her skin is tan. I think she might be part African American and part white, but she never said anything to me about her race. Mr. Sylvester looks very white, with pinkish skin and a big nose. What will people think when they see the two of them with a Chinese baby? Then I remember what my mother says: *Don't worry about what other people think or what race they are. People are people.*

Mr. Sylvester is reading a book called *Lucky Girl* about a baby who was adopted from China. Lucky Family Orphanage. *Lucky Girl.* Funny how things associated with adoption are called lucky. But nobody talks about the unlucky families who gave their baby girls away.

I open the journal Camille gave me, and on the first page in her perfect handwriting she wrote:

To my best friend,
Anna. Love, Camille

I write the date:

Dec. 12
I hope my suitcase is on this plane. What
if fifty hats get lost?

I draw little hats all around the border of the page and then close my journal. I want to open the blue envelope from Andee, but she said to wait until I'm actually in China. I feel tired and jittery at the same time, and my legs are numb. It is dark outside. Soon Mr. Sylvester is snoring and I wish I were home in my bed with Maow Maow.

All night people are coming and going. A flight attendant brings a hot meal, but I'm not hungry and the smell turns my stomach. Later she brings orange juice. People are laughing and playing cards. I close my eyes.

Our plane lands in Japan and we have to hurry to catch our next flight. I follow Ms. Sylvester's green sweater through the crowded airport, where I see more people with black hair than I've ever seen before. We get to the gate just in time, and finally we are on the plane to Beijing.

"I'm getting butterflies in my stomach," Ms. Sylvester says.

Mr. Sylvester puts his arm around her. "Everything will be fine. You'll see."

She takes out the itinerary that was given to her by the adoption agency. First we will go to the hotel and get settled in. The next day, we have a tour of the Great Wall. The second day is the Forbidden City. "I wish we didn't have to do so much sightseeing before we get Jing," she says.

"You know what the lady told us. They want us to get an appreciation for China before we get our babies," Mr. Sylvester says.

She sighs and leans back on his arm. "How are you doing, Anna?"

"Fine."

"Another couple of hours and we'll be there," she says.

I close my eyes for a minute and listen to the voices of the people on the plane. Most people are talking in Chinese, but I hear English, too. I cannot imagine hearing only Chinese all around me. What if I can't understand a thing in Beijing?

"What do you think were the biggest challenges for your family when you got Kaylee?" Mr. Sylvester asks.

"She cried a lot, and she had an eating problem," I say. "But now she eats just fine." I think about my sister eating Cheerios and laughing, and suddenly I am so homesick that I can hardly stand it.

"That must have been so hard for all of you," Ms. Sylvester says.

"But look at her now," Mr. Sylvester says. "Not a thing wrong with her." He opens his wallet and takes out a picture of Jing. "And not a thing wrong with her, either."

"We don't know yet, Roy," Ms. Sylvester says. "Every baby is different."

When we get off the plane, a thin lady in a blue suit meets our group. "Follow me," she says in English. We pile into a van. "Welcome to Beijing." She has to shout over the noise of the engine. "We hope you will enjoy China." The sun is just setting and it's hard to see anything except the outline of the skyscrapers. She points out sights as we cross the city, and talks about the way the roads are organized in rings from the center out. "Now we are at the third ring road," she says.

I am so tired that I can't pay attention. When we get to the hotel, I stumble into the lobby and we make our way to our room on the second floor.

The last thing I think of as I am falling asleep is the gold carpet.

Chapter Eleven

Sightseeing

Where is Maow Maow and where is my desk? I hear Mr. Sylvester snoring and I realize that I am not at home. The clock says 1:04 a.m.

My stomach is growling, so I reach for the trail mix in the pocket of my backpack. I eat the raisins first, then the peanuts and the M&M's. If I were at home, I would be having Cheerios and milk. No, China is thirteen hours ahead, so at home it is two in the afternoon. I would be in math class. I wish I had something cold and juicy, like an apple. I want to read but the light might wake up the Sylvesters. I tiptoe into the bathroom, turn on the light, and start reading *Homesick*. The author was born in China but she is

American. I never really thought of what it would be like to be a white American kid who grew up in China speaking Chinese better than English. Like me, only in reverse. I read half of the book before the sky becomes light.

Finally a little bit of pink sunshine comes in through the small window. I can't believe I am more than six thousand miles from Cincin-

nati. At home, Ken and Kaylee and Mom and Dad are probably finishing dinner. Laura and Camille are doing their homework. Maybe Andee is in her art cove, making earrings. Tears come to my eyes. I miss home so much already. How will I last for twelve whole days? Then I remember the blue envelope.

Inside is a card:

Dear Anna, I wanted to make you fortune cookies, but knew they'd get crushed,

so here are twelve paper ones. Open one
each day that you are in China.
Love, Andee.

P.S. I hope my fortunes make more sense
than the ones in real fortune cookies!

Inside the card are twelve different-colored folded
circles of paper held together with a purple paper clip.
Each paper cookie has a number on it. I open the first
one and find this fortune inside:

You have jet lag, but you will
have a great time in China. 你好

In the corner, Andee has written the Chinese characters for Ni hao. I refold the paper fortune cookie and
put everything back into the envelope. Andee thought
of the perfect gift.

When the Sylvesters wake up, we take showers and
get dressed. I put on a sweater and a jacket because it

is cold even in the hotel. The guide who met us yesterday is waiting in the lobby. She speaks English, but sometimes it's hard to understand because her voice rises and falls at the wrong times. I think she's explaining that breakfast is included with our hotel fee. We go into the other room, where we each get a bowl of rice cooked in broth with salty pickles. It feels good on my dry throat.

After breakfast, Ms. Sylvester explains to the guide that before the babies arrive, we would like to visit the Lucky Family Orphanage.

"I don't understand," she says.

Ms. Sylvester puts her arm around me. "This is Anna. She has a sister who was adopted from the Lucky Family Orphanage, the same orphanage as our daughter, Jing. We would like to visit."

"I don't think that is possible," she says. "We have a schedule for every day."

"It is very important," Ms. Sylvester says.

The guide says she understands, but she doesn't say that she will try to arrange something. Outside it is cold and gray and the air smells like gasoline and smoke. I wind my scarf around my neck and pull my hat down over my ears. The lady calls the van, and we are on our way to the Great Wall. Through the dirty van windows, I see lots of billboards with huge red Chinese characters on them, and more cranes than I've ever seen in one place. The lady is pointing out some sights, but I'm too tired to concentrate and the ride is long and bumpy. I close my eyes.

When we stop, I see big groups of tourists talking in different languages. There are Chinese tour groups too, and when they are speaking Mandarin, I can understand some of the words. We join the crowds all bundled up against the wind and start walking up the hill on top of the wall, which is wide, like a road made of stones and bricks. It's hard to imagine how anyone could have built something this big and this long without machinery. At home we have a picture book with paintings that show strong men carrying huge stones to form the base of the wall. Many people died while carrying these heavy stones. But the guide doesn't say anything about that. She explains that the Chinese were very advanced in their knowledge of construction. The Great Wall was built as a fortress to protect from invaders, and it was meant to last forever.

I take pictures and so do all the other families. The guide tells us that the Great Wall is the only man-made structure visible from outer space. I try to imagine looking down on earth from the moon and seeing the wall, but my head will not stop spinning.

Finally we stop for lunch at a noodle restaurant, where all the customers and servers are Asian except for the Sylvesters and the other white couples in our group. I see our wait-

ress stare at Mr. Sylvester's big nose, but he doesn't seem to notice. After lunch, I buy a few postcards at a kiosk. The guide wants us to continue our tour, but we are so tired that we ask if we can go back to the hotel.

The Sylvesters lie down for a nap, but even though I'm exhausted, I can't sleep. I take my green journal and go down to the lobby by myself. A teenager who is not much taller than me and dressed in a waitress uniform says something to me in Chinese, but I can't understand. I ask her to repeat please, and the second time I think that she is asking if I am hungry.

"*Chi bao le*," I say, meaning that I'm full.

She smiles. "You are adopted?" she asks in English.

"No."

She looks confused. I realize that I'd better learn how to explain who I am in Chinese. "I was born in America. Now I came to China with my teacher to get a Chinese baby." I realize I've never said this much in Chinese before. Then in English I say, "My *mei mei* was adopted."

The waitress says something about many families in America who adopt Chinese babies. I can't tell from her face if she thinks that is a good thing or not. I want to ask her more, but she is cleaning the tables, plus I don't know how to say very much in Chinese. She stops for a minute. "Teach your *mei mei* Chinese language," she says. "This is very important."

I nod.

"You, too. Then you and your *mei mei* can come back." She picks up a paper menu. "You can read this."

I recognize some of the characters, like the ones for fruit and meat and noodles.

"Very good," she says. "I can be your teacher in China." She hands me the menu. "For you. Write. I can check later."

I sit in one of the stuffed chairs that smell like ciga-rettes and copy the characters from the menu into my journal. Next to the ones I know, I write the definitions in English, but jet lag is making everything spin — the words on my paper, the lights, the desk, the gold car-pet. A lady is sweeping the floor and another is dust-ing the desk. A man is washing the windows. All of them are Chinese like me. But I don't know them and they don't know me and I can't understand them well. The smell of the cleaning supplies makes me feel nau-seated. I wish I could go home and smell Kaylee's baby shampoo and Mom's anise beef and Grandma's sea-weed soup that I love.

Chapter Twelve
The Waitress

The next morning, I open Fortune Cookie 2:

> You will make a
> friend in China.　　朋友

In the corner are the Chinese characters for *peng you*, "friend." How can I make a friend in China when I'm not going to school and there are no other kids in the hotel? Could the waitress be my new *peng you*?

Our group spends most of the day in the Forbidden City. There's an outer court and an inner court, hundreds of buildings, and a museum. I like the fancy tiles and sculptures, but my legs get really tired. Finally we sit down in a restaurant and have steamed dumplings, which are delicious. The server asks if we'd like forks or chopsticks, and Mr. Sylvester chooses chopsticks, but then he has no idea how to use them. I show him the way Mom taught us. You hold the bottom chopstick still and move the top one close to it to pick things up. But when Mr. Sylvester tries, the dumpling explodes on his lap. I try not to laugh. When I look at Ms. Sylvester, she is covering her mouth with a napkin.

In the evening, I manage to tell the story to the waitress at our hotel, half in English and half in Chinese.

"He needs special chopsticks for babies," she says. "I can show you." She goes to the back of the restaurant and comes back with plastic chopsticks that are tied together with a rubber band and have elephants on top. Thinking about Mr. Sylvester eating with elephant chopsticks makes me start laughing all over again. Maybe jet lag is making me giddy.

※ ※ ※

Fortune Cookie 3 is purple.

You are having fun! 中国

In the corner are the characters for *Zhong guo*, "China." I think about that for a minute. Being in China isn't that easy. First I had jet lag, and now my legs are tired from sightseeing. I also feel homesick, especially at night. But laughing with the waitress is fun. And somehow I really like walking around in China and feeling like I don't stand out.

The Summer Palace has a pretty lake and gardens with small stone bridges. The weather is cold, but the sun is shining and I take lots of pictures. I buy postcards for Mom and Mrs. Smith and Ms. Remick. When we get back to the hotel, Ms. Sylvester reminds the guide again that we would like to go to the Lucky Family Orphanage.

"This is not easy to arrange," she says. "I will try."

"Thank you. It is very important," Ms. Sylvester says again.

In the evening, the waitress sits down at a table next to me. I tell her that we want to visit my sister's orphanage, but it seems like it might be impossible.

"Why do you want to go there?" she asks. "An orphanage is sad—so many babies with no parents."

I try to explain in Chinese that I want to learn more about my sister, but she doesn't understand. I try again in English, but that doesn't work either.

"I know," she says finally. "You love your sister."

"Yes," I say.

She takes a bag of candy out of her pocket. "For your family," she says. "My little brother likes this kind."

I'm surprised that she has a brother, because I thought you were only allowed to have one child in China, but I don't say anything. "Maybe you should give the candy to him," I say.

"I have more for my brother." She takes out her phone and shows me a picture of a wiry boy with big ears. "We call him little monkey," she says. "He is very funny."

"Wait," I say. I run up to my room to get the photo album. I show the waitress pictures of Mom, Dad,

Ken, and Kaylee. She spends a long time looking at each photo.

"You have a nice family and a big house," she says. "We live in one room. Maybe you can visit."

"I would like that," I say.

"I will tell my mother." She smiles. "She is a very good cook." She looks at the clock. "Now I have to go home." She drops her phone into her purse, puts on her jacket, and heads out into the wind. When she gets to the end of the walk, she turns and waves to me.

Chapter Thirteen

So Many Fortunes

Each morning, I open another paper fortune cookie. Fortune Cookie 4 is pink:

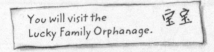

You will visit the Lucky Family Orphanage. 宝宝

Andee has written the Chinese characters for *bao bao,* "baby." This time I think her fortune might be wrong. The guide has not reported any progress, and each time we ask, she just tells us to be patient.

We spend the day at the Beijing Zoo. I love the giant pandas, especially the cubs. Two of them wrestle and roll around, then get tired and curl up for a nap. Watching them makes me miss Ken and Kaylee so much. I wonder what they are doing at home without me.

I have to use the bathroom. The toilets in China are really weird, with two places for your feet and a hole in the ground, so you have to squat, which means you have to practically get undressed and freeze each time you pee. I wonder if Mom grew up with toilets like these.

Fortune Cookie 5 is blue:

Your Chinese is getting better. 中国话

She wrote the characters for "Chinese language," *Zhong guo hua.* I'm not really sure if that's true. Sometimes the sentences come to me without thinking, and other times I stumble over every word. At the Lama Temple, I ask a lady where the bathroom is and she has no trouble understanding me, but when I try to explain to the temple tour guide that I am from America, which is why I don't speak Chinese very well, she stares at me with a blank face and says, "A Chinese face but no Chinese words." Then she shakes her head. I wish I could explain to her that I'm trying really hard to learn and I know a lot more than I used to, but her stern face makes me wish I could disappear into my puffy jacket.

Fortune Cookie 6 is metallic gold.

Andee drew a calendar and shaded in two weeks. It's hard to believe that my stay in China really is half over. In some ways it seems as if I've been in China much longer than a week, but in other ways, it feels as if I just got here.

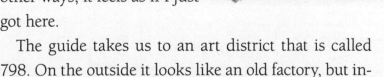

The guide takes us to an art district that is called 798. On the outside it looks like an old factory, but inside are exhibits that are different from anything I've ever seen. There's a giant red hand making a fist, and a car covered in silver. Mr. Sylvester says he is not interested in this kind of art, and he complains that it is too cold and drafty. Ms. Sylvester tells him to sit down in a café and she takes my arm. "Let's explore, Anna," she says. We look at all the stores selling T-shirts with really cool designs. Ms. Sylvester buys some that she says are for her nieces and nephews, but when we leave, she hands one to me. "A memory of our girls' day out," she says, smiling. It has a picture of the Beijing skyline on the front, and on the back it just has the numbers 798 and the Chinese characters for Beijing.

Fortune Cookie 7 is white:

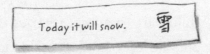

Today it will snow. 雪

Andee wrote the Chinese character *xue* for "snow." I wonder if her mother showed her how to write all these Chinese characters. Outside the sky is white, with a few flurries blowing around. Maybe Andee looked up the ten-day weather forecast for Beijing. But then the sun comes out and the weather feels warmer than usual.

We spend the day visiting the old part of Beijing. The *hu tong* houses are made out of little buildings all connected, with a courtyard in the middle. They were built like that for big families, the guide explains. The grandparents live in one part, and each of the children has another. I would love to live in one of these. Grandma could be on one side, and Mom and Dad and Ken and Kaylee and me in the middle. The third side could be for Mom's family. Grandma Wai Po could have a quiet room facing the courtyard, and her brothers and sisters and their families could have the other rooms. Then I could play with my cousins every day. Suddenly I wish Mom were here and we really could go to Shanghai. I know I have some cousins there who are around my age, but I can't remember if they are boys or girls, and I don't even know their names.

An old lady comes out of one of the houses to feed the fish in a big fishbowl near the door. She looks around and her eyes land on me. She motions for me to come close. I look inside and see two big goldfish swimming around. She shows me how to sprinkle the fish food on top of the water. Then she pats my head and goes back into the house. I wonder if she thinks I am a girl from Beijing.

Fortune Cookie 8 just has a bunch of little icicles. Andee is right: it got colder again. After eight days of sightseeing, we are getting tired of the weather and the traffic that never stops and the pollution that stings our eyes. Nobody in our adoption group wants to go anywhere else, and the people are starting to get irritable. One couple tells the guide that they aren't going on tomorrow's tour, and she seems annoyed. "You

must know China," she says. "How can you receive a baby and not know where she comes from? Tomorrow we meet here and go to the art museum."

"What about the Lucky Family Orphanage?" Ms. Sylvester asks.

"Please be patient," the guide says.

I'm tired of sightseeing too, but I'm starting to get used to walking though crowded streets full of people and vendors and bicycles. Sometimes I wish I could leave the group and go by myself so nobody would think I am American. I can feel my Chinese getting better. Yesterday I asked a lady for a bag of lemon candy and she understood me right away. Ms. Sylvester was impressed. "If only I could do that," she said.

Chapter Fourteen

A Visit

Mr. Sylvester doesn't like the coffee in the hotel, so he wants to go find a Starbucks. Ms. Sylvester wants to stay in the hotel room and write down the day's events. "Someday I want to tell Jing about our trip," she says.

Mr. Sylvester paces in the small room. "This place is so . . ." he looks around the room. "So dingy."

"Roy, there is nothing wrong with this room, or with the coffee either." Ms. Sylvester glares at him, then turns back to her notebook.

He stands by the window, gazing out onto the city. I know he is thinking that Beijing is polluted. And he's right. You can see a brown haze all the way to the horizon, and my eyes burn when I am outside for a long time. But I love the way old people gather in the parks to exercise and play mahjong and watch their grand-children. I like the way kids my age and even younger go everywhere on buses without adults. And China is the country that Kaylee and the Sylvesters' daughter will always be from, no matter how long they live in America.

China is also the place where my mom was born. Maybe now that I've spent time here, she'll tell me more about her life. And I'll know what kinds of questions to ask. Did she grow up in a high-rise apartment? Did she have cousins close by? Did she walk to school or take a bus? When she tells me the answers, I'll be able to imagine the crowded streets and a bus so full that people are hanging on to the door handles.

Mr. Sylvester is still pacing. I go downstairs to find the waitress. As soon as she sees me, she smiles. "I wait for you," she says in English. She gives me a bag with three coloring books. In Chinese, she explains that she knows I am too old for coloring, but they have lots of good vocabulary words, like *cao mei,* which is a kind of fruit. She goes into the kitchen and comes back with a small bowl full of red fuzzy fruit I've never seen before. It has a prickly texture, but the taste is a little like a strawberry, just more sour. At first it makes my mouth pucker, but then I like it.

She asks me if I can teach her some English.

"What's your name?" I ask her in English.

"My name is Fan," she says. Her pronunciation in English is slow and clear.

"My name is Anna."

I write down a list of fruit: *strawberry, apple, orange, banana,* and draw little pictures next to each one. She repeats the words very well. "Thank you," she says. "Someday I can visit you?"

"Yes," I say, smiling. "You can visit my home."

"Today can you come to my home? I am finished with my work."

"I'll go check," I say.

Ms. Sylvester comes down

to talk to Fan. She says she lives not too far away, only fifteen minutes by bus. Fan puts her arm around me and says that she is almost sixteen years old, and she will take care of me like her *xiao mei,* little sister. For a minute I wish that she really were my big sister and that we could talk every day for the rest of my life.

The bus is so full that Fan has to push me on. I don't think I've ever been in such a crowded space in my life, but she doesn't seem to think there is anything unusual. More people get on at each stop until we are pressed together like sardines. It smells like wet wool and damp shoes. The bus gets on the highway.

We have to fight our way through the people to get off, and I step down into a big mud puddle.

"Sorry," Fan says. "The street is in bad condition." She takes my hand and pulls me along. A truck goes by and splashes us. Fan tries to brush off my jacket.

It starts to rain. The sky is almost dark, and the air smells like gasoline and charcoal. We turn down an alley and wind our way behind some buildings. "This is my home," she says finally, opening a door with her key.

Inside the light is dim. Her brother is watching television and her mother is cooking on a hot plate. "This is my friend from America," Fan says.

Her mother looks up at me. She and Fan have similar smiles. Then she says something that I don't understand to Fan, who gets a bowl. Her mother fills it with dumplings for me.

"*Xie xie,*" I say. Thank you.

"Does she speak Chinese?" her mom asks Fan, not realizing that I understand.

"Yes. I am her teacher." Fan turns to me and speaks in Chinese. "My mother makes the best dumplings. My aunt says her dumplings are better, but it's not true."

I taste one and the flavor of ginger fills my mouth. "Very delicious," I say. I eat the rest and Fan refills my bowl.

Her mother smiles. "You are a hungry girl."

"Your dumplings are very good." I turn to Fan, and in English I say, "I wish your mom could teach my mom how to make these dumplings." Fan translates for her mom.

"Bring your mom to China and I will teach her," she says.

Fan speaks to me slowly and clearly in simple Chinese. "This is our room. The rest of our family is still back home."

"Where is that?" I ask.

"One day on the train," she says. "In the country-side. Only we came to Beijing."

I want to ask Fan why they left the countryside to come to this tiny room in this enormous city, but I don't know enough Chinese to ask all that. In the back of the room are three beds, one single and two bunks. A poster of roses is taped to the wall. Fan gets a small album and shows me pictures of her and her brother in a big park. "Beijing is nice in summer. Can you come back?"

"Maybe someday."

Her brother comes over to see. "This is Anna," Fan tells him. She turns to me. "He is naughty. He only wants to watch TV."

The boy goes back to his cartoons. Fan's mother smooths my hair. "You speak Chinese very well," she says.

"*Yi dian dian*," I say. A little bit.

"Are your mother and your father from Beijing?"

I shake my head. "My father is from America and my mother is from Shanghai."

"Shanghai is very beautiful," Fan's mother says. "I saw pictures, but it is too far to travel."

"I have a big family there," I say. I want to tell her that we plan to visit in a couple of years, but I am getting really tired from speaking so much Chinese.

Fan shows me more pictures of her friends and her cousins. Then we play a game of concentration with her brother, who beats us both. "He has a good memory," she says.

The boy laughs. "You forget too much."

She rubs his short hair. And then it is time to go.

The bus is not as crowded now, and we sit together on a seat. "I think your home in America is not like mine," she says.

"My home is bigger," I admit. "But my brother is like yours. He likes cartoons and he has big ears. He has a good memory too, but sometimes I can beat him in card games."

She smiles. "I hope we can go to America someday. My brother can be friends with your brother."

"I like your home," I say. "Thank you for taking me."

We are quiet then, leaning against each other as the bus goes over potholes and gravel. I wish Fan and her family lived as close to me as Laura and her mom.

Chapter Fifteen

Alone

In the morning, like she does every day, Ms. Sylvester asks our guide about visiting the orphanage.

"We have to wait and see," she says.

"We only have three more days in China," Ms. Sylvester reminds her.

I open Fortune Cookie 9, which is red:

> Good Luck will continue to be with you for the last quarter of your trip and the rest of your life.

She wrote the Chinese characters for "good luck" on the back.

❈ ❈ ❈

Finally, after so many days of sightseeing, we have a Sunday off, and the babies are coming on Monday. Ms. Sylvester checks the adoption forms over and over to make sure everything is in order.

"They would have told us if they weren't," Mr. Sylvester says.

"Not necessarily," Ms. Sylvester says. "It never hurts to check."

I sit on my bed and open Fortune Cookie 10:

Andee drew a little smiley face and the characters for "child," *xiao hai*. What if Baby Jing cries all day and all night and there is nothing we can do? Mom said Kaylee was like that. But not all babies that come from China are fussy. I slip out the door and down the stairs. Fan is not in the lobby. I open the door of the hotel, and for the first time, I go out by myself in China.

The smell of wood fires used to grill meat combined

with car exhaust is familiar by now. I walk past the small park where I always see the same old man doing slow exercises. He smiles at me and I smile back. Here nobody stares at me. They assume that I live in one of these apartment buildings with my parents and that I go to the school down the street and buy lunch from the vendors in the square.

I turn the corner and walk past the playground. A lady is there with her grandson. "*Xiao xin*," she tells

him, be careful, as she pushes his swing. He holds the chains with mittened hands and laughs. A man and his granddaughter are tossing a ball. She misses and it rolls toward me. I pick it up and gently toss it to her.

I sit down on the bench. Here I am, an ordinary girl sitting on a bench at a playground in Beijing. More people are coming to exercise and walk in the park. A woman is leading a group of other women in tai chi. They move slowly with their knees bent. One of them is stocky with short hair. For a second I think she is Grandma and begin to imagine really living here. I would probably go to the elementary school at the end of the block and wear a blue skirt and a white blouse with a red kerchief around my neck like the two girls walking toward me. They look around my age. If I lived here, maybe they would be my friends.

I realize that I didn't tell the Sylvesters I was leaving the hotel. What if they are looking for me? I hurry out of the park, around the block, and back into the warmth of the lobby. Quickly I run up the stairs to our room.

They did not even notice I was gone.

In my journal I write:

Who Am I?
I am from a playground in China
where a little boy swings
and old people
do tai chi
under the trees
in winter.

I close the notebook and lean my head against the back of the sofa. I feel really tired for some reason. I wish I were home in our living room with Kaylee and Ken bickering the way they do, and Mom and Dad in the kitchen. I wish I could call Camille and Laura and Andee. I want to tell them about China, but then I'm not really sure what I would say.

I look around at the hotel lobby with its smoke-stained walls and gold carpet. In some ways it feels so familiar to me now. Soon Fan will come and tell me about her little monkey brother and what her mom cooked for dinner. I will teach her new words in English and she will teach me new words in Chinese. We will laugh together. Maybe we can go out and buy some candy at the little corner store.

It's strange to think that I've been away for only ten days. I feel as if I've been here much longer. And I still have not been able to visit the orphanage. What if I don't get permission and I have to bring all the hats back? Everyone in CAT will be so disappointed. But no matter what happens, I am really, really glad I decided to come to China.

Chapter Sixteen
The Babies

Each caregiver carries one baby. We watch as they make their way from the van into the hotel lobby, where we have been instructed to wait.

The guide has a list of names and she calls the couples one at a time. "Victor and Susan Brown."

The couple goes to meet their baby.

"Sylvan and Victoria Holiman," "Nathalie Kamensky and Jason Lees," "Suzanne and Roy Sylvester."

Mr. and Ms. Sylvester move toward a short lady who is holding a baby. I follow behind. The lady hands the baby to Ms. Sylvester. She has big dark eyes and a wide forehead. The baby stares at Ms. Sylvester's face for a minute, then reaches for her necklace. Ms. Sylvester

has tears running down her cheeks. Mr. Sylvester is still holding her around her shoulders. Baby Jing makes a cooing noise as she shakes the necklace. Ms. Sylvester kisses the baby's cheek and then hands her to Mr. Sylvester. Jing stares at his face and grabs his nose.

He laughs. "It's a big one, isn't it?"

Then she wants the necklace again.

The room is noisy with babies cooing and crying and people talking. Mom and Dad said Kaylee screamed for hours when they first got her, but most of these babies seem pretty calm. Now Jing is playing with the buttons on Mr. Sylvester's sweater.

The guide folds her list of names, and the caregivers

are turning to leave in the van. "Say goodbye, Jing," Ms. Sylvester says.

The caregiver is patting Jing's back. "*Hen hao de bao bao*," she says. "*Mei wen ti.*"

I translate. "A very good baby. No problem."

"I wish you could stay longer," Ms. Sylvester says.

"*Deng yi deng,* Can you wait?" I ask.

The lady shakes her head. She pats Jing once more on her head, then turns to go.

"*Zai jian,*" I say, holding Jing's arm to help her wave.

But Jing is too interested in the buttons on Mr. Sylvester's sweater to say goodbye.

The guide comes over to me. "Tomorrow we can go to the orphanage. I will be here at nine in the morning."

"We will be ready," Ms. Sylvester says.

"Only Anna," the guide says. "That is the permission that I got."

Ms. Sylvester looks worried. "By herself?"

"I'll be fine," I say.

"Tomorrow, nine o'clock, in the lobby," the guide repeats. "I wait for you."

"*Xie xie,*" I say, feeling excited and scared at the same time.

We take Jing up to our hotel room and set her on the bed. She looks around at everything, and then reaches for Ms. Sylvester.

"Mama," Mr. Sylvester says.

Jing watches his mouth like Kaylee used to.

"Daddy," Ms. Sylvester says, pointing to her husband.

"*Ba ba,*" I say, in Chinese. Daddy.

Mr. Sylvester looks at me. "Anna. Can you say Anna?"

Jing is busy playing with the chain hanging on the lamp.

"She seems to like shiny things," Ms. Sylvester says.

Mr. Sylvester drops his keys on the bed. Jing picks them up, shakes them, and smiles at the sound.

When she gets fussy, Ms. Sylvester mixes up some formula and gives it to Baby Jing in a bottle. She sucks hard and soon the bottle is empty. Mr. Sylvester burps her and changes her wet diaper. Then Mr. Sylvester wants to take her for a walk, but Ms. Sylvester says it's too soon, they should just get used to each other for now.

"She is already used to us," Mr. Sylvester says.

It seems like he's right. Jing smiles and coos and eats and burps just like she's supposed to. Around seven thirty she starts rubbing her eyes and yawning. They lay her down in the collapsible baby bed, and she sucks her thumb quietly.

"Easy," Mr. Sylvester whispers.

"Just wait," Ms. Sylvester says. "Babies go through stages."

"Well, the first one is great!" he says.

Mr. and Ms. Sylvester are sitting together, staring at Jing as she falls asleep.

I go down to the lobby to look for Fan, but she's not there. One of the couples is walking back and forth with their baby, who just won't stop crying. The man keeps jiggling her up and down, but still she screams. They look exhausted.

"When my parents first adopted my sister, she cried a lot too," I say. "It helped if I sang to her."

The mom looks at me and I see the deep circles around her eyes. The baby is quiet for a moment. Then she lets out a scream even louder than Kaylee's. "Do you want to try?" the lady asks, handing the baby to me.

"What's her name?" I ask.

"Susan," the lady says.

I take Susan, sit on the sofa, and start singing the tiger song that Kaylee likes. As soon as I get to the end, I

start over. At first Susan still screams, but then she takes longer between cries and I can tell that she is listening. "*Liang zhi lao hu,*" I sing again.

I sing the fruit song and the gumdrops song and "Twinkle Twinkle." As long as I sing, she doesn't cry. The man joins in. "Twinkle, twinkle, little Susan," he croons. We sing it three times, and then Susan is asleep.

"You really know how to settle her down," the lady says. "We can't thank you enough."

I put Baby Susan in her stroller. She sticks her fist in her mouth and keeps on sleeping.

"Do you think you can teach us the Chinese song?" the lady asks.

I try to teach them the first verse of the tiger song. They don't know any Chinese, so it sounds pretty funny, but maybe Susan will recognize the tune.

When I go back up to my room, all three Sylvesters are sound asleep.

Chapter Seventeen

The Lucky Family Orphanage

The sun is just starting to rise. I get up quietly and fill my backpack with all the hats, along with my camera and the small photo album. I put the fortune cookie money in an inside zippered pocket. The Sylvesters are still asleep. Baby Jing is in her bed. Her eyes are halfway open and she is quietly sucking her thumb.

I go down to the lobby and wait. When the guide comes, we run out to the curb and she hails a taxi. The traffic is terrible, and cars and bicycles and people are everywhere. The taxi driver keeps honking for people to move out of the way. The guide is arguing with him about the best way to get to the orphanage. I can understand some words like "left" and "right," but they are talking really fast. The driver asks the lady if I was adopted from the Lucky Family Orphanage and she says yes.

"My sister was adopted, not me," I say in English.

She doesn't translate for the taxi driver. He swerves around a big hole in the street, honks, and takes off down the highway. On the shoulder there are three-wheeled bicycles piled high with vegetables and bottles of water and cardboard boxes. We go over a big bump and I feel yesterday's dinner in my throat.

Finally we exit and drive down a gravel road for about twenty minutes. Then we turn the corner and I see it, just like on the website: a gray two-story building with a big sign in front that says LUCKY FAMILY ORPHANAGE in red characters. The taxi driver stops, the lady pays him, and we step out into a wind so cold, it takes my breath away.

First we go into an office. The lady sitting behind the desk asks who we are, and our guide explains something very fast. I want to tell her that my sister was adopted from this orphanage, but she is busy with the forms and motions for us to sit down on two chairs.

I put my head back against the wall and hear the sounds of voices and crying. The lady turns on a radio and it plays American pop music. She prints out more forms, which the guide fills out. Then the lady calls over a man, who points to various things on the form. Could there be a problem? They argue for a minute. Finally the lady says, "Come along," in English.

We follow her down a hallway and into a room she calls the baby room, with windows along one wall. The sun is shining right into my eyes and for a few moments I can't see anything. Then there they are, rows of small cribs and ladies with white smocks going from one to another. Some babies are sitting, some are standing, others are sleeping. "*Zao an*," a lady says. Good morning.

"*Zao an*," I reply.

The orphanage lady talks to a person who is sitting at a desk in the back of the room. I think she is explaining that my baby sister was adopted from this orphanage two years ago. The two of them keep looking at me.

I take the photo album out of my backpack and open it to a picture of Kaylee when she first arrived.

The lady takes the album and calls to some of the other women. They crowd around the photo album.

Suddenly they are all talking at once. "Of course, look at our Bao Bao, she is so big," one says.

"*Hen piao liang*," says another. "Very pretty." She calls more ladies over.

"Look, come and see our Bao Bao."

"Does she still cry so much?"

"Is she eating better now?"

I smile. These ladies knew my sister very well. They held her and rocked her and tried to comfort her.

"She eats now," I say. The Chinese words are flowing easily. "She likes bananas and hamburgers. And she loves to play with our cat." I show them the picture of Kaylee with Maow Maow.

One of the ladies laughs. "Our Bao Bao is chasing a cat," she says.

They look through all the pictures and say that our house is so beautiful. I want to take pictures of the ladies and the babies, but the guide says I am not allowed, so I put the camera away. Some babies wave to me. Others are sleeping. One is crying and a lady is patting her on the back.

Then one of the women who is younger than the

others talks to me in English. "I remember your *mei mei*. A crying baby," she says, and I see that her eyes are watery. "Bao Bao likes songs."

"Especially the one about the two tigers," I say.

"I used to sing to her." She switches to Chinese. "Bao Bao is very stubborn."

"Yes," I say, showing her the picture of Kaylee pulling her mouse away from the cat.

"She has a strong personality," she says.

"That's good," another lady says. "Especially for a girl."

"Do you remember the day she came here?" I ask.

The ladies look at each other. An older lady clears her throat and talks in a mixture of Chinese and English. "It was raining that day, and cold, too. Windy, like today. A lady who works in that office there—see it out the window? That one there on the end of the road? She found a baby wrapped in a blanket right there on the steps. She said she almost stepped over it, but because the baby was crying, she stopped. Then she brought the baby to us before she went to her work." She looks at the babies in the cribs. "Many of our babies are found like this."

"Do you know who that lady is?" I ask.

"There are lots of ladies who work there. It is a big office. They are accountants, I think, for all these factories." She makes a gesture with her arm.

"Did she ever come again, I mean, to see Bao Bao?" I know my Chinese is full of mistakes, but they seem to understand.

The lady shakes her head. "No. She didn't come back."

"A crying baby is lucky," the younger lady says. "If she didn't cry, maybe the lady wouldn't see her, and she would just step over that bundle on the steps."

The older lady smiles. "She is happy now, our Bao Bao."

"My parents said that a man brought Bao Bao to them at the hotel. Is he here?"

The ladies look at each other. "We had a man who worked here before. But now he moved," the older one says. "He went to his family."

"Can we find him?'

She shakes her head. "It is far away. We cannot go there."

"I have something for the babies," I say. "From my school." I take my backpack off my back and empty it onto a table.

"So many hats!" a lady says, holding them up one at a time.

"Such beautiful colors," another one says.

"Many students at my school made them. A teacher, too." I show them the picture of CAT and wish so much that Andee and Sam and Simone and everyone else were here with me.

One lady picks out a blue hat with a yellow pom-pom and puts it onto a baby's head. I think it is the hat that Sam knitted, because some of the stitches are too loose. Then they all start putting the hats on the babies. A lady laughs. "Like little snowmen," she says.

I clear my throat. "My school also raised money for the babies."

"We have everything," one lady says.

I look around the room. It's true, they have stacks of diapers and cans of formula and small cribs with sheets, but in the whole room, there are no baby toys.

I reach for my backpack, take out the envelope with the money, and hand it to the young lady. "Please buy toys or whatever you need for the babies," I say. "A present from my school."

The lady doesn't understand.

"At my school we had a bake sale," I say. "This money is for the Lucky Family Orphanage."

I'm not sure she understands what a bake sale is. But she understands that the money is a gift. "*Xie xie,*" she says. "To all the students and the teachers."

I want to tell her about CAT and the fortune cookies. But I cannot possibly explain all that in Chinese. Plus the babies are starting to get fussy. They need bottles and diaper changes and songs.

Just when the guide says it is time to leave, I remember Kaylee's drawing and take it out of my backpack. "Bao Bao drew this for you," I say, giving it to the young woman. Then I hand her the photo album. "So you can remember my sister."

Chapter Eighteen
A Fever

When I get back to the hotel room, the Sylvesters are not there. They left a note on my bed: *Hope the visit went well. Gone out for a bit, back soon.*

I know I should write down everything that happened at the orphanage, but I feel exhausted. I open my backpack to take out a bottle of water. Then I see that one baby hat must have gotten stuck in the zipper. Should I give it to the guide and ask her to take it to the orphanage? But she would have no reason to go back.

I feel too tired to write or read, so I reach for the blue envelope and carefully unfold the eleventh fortune cookie, which is white:

There is a picture of a house and the Chinese characters *hui jia,* "back home."

It's true. In just a couple of days, we will be on the plane again, this time with Jing. I lie down on my bed, close my eyes, and watch the colors swirling behind my eyelids, red and blue and pink and green, like millions of baby hats and pompoms and traffic.

Suddenly I remember the oral history project. In all my excitement about the orphanage, I forgot to actually interview anyone. How could I have forgotten something so important? What will I tell Ms. Remick and Mrs. Smith?

I wake up many times during the night and I hear Jing, but then I fall asleep again. When I look at the clock, it is almost two thirty a.m. I can hear Mr.

Sylvester snoring in the other room. Jing moves in her baby bed. I reach for my flashlight and open my journal:

All night I dreamed about the orphanage.
I cannot stop thinking about it. I wonder
who will adopt the other babies. If nobody
does, where will they go? I forgot to ask
the ladies so many things. And I forgot

to interview someone for the oral history
project.

I wish I could magically just be home
in my own bed. I miss everybody so much.
And I don't feel very good.

I put the notebook down, and the room is spinning.
My throat hurts. I turn toward the wall and close my
eyes.

Day and night are the same and the room is hot and
Jing cries and stops and cries and stops. Mr. Sylvester
snores and Ms. Sylvester brings me water that is cool
on my dry lips, but it hurts to swallow. I'm thirsty, so
I have to drink, and I have to sleep to make the room
stop spinning.

In the middle of the night, I open my eyes and everything is still. My stomach feels empty. There are a
few crackers next to my bed, so I eat those and wait
for six o'clock, because that's when they put out the
breakfast downstairs in the hotel.

I get dressed as quietly as I can, take my journal,

and tiptoe out of the room and down the stairs. The breakfast is out but there is nobody in the room except me. I have a bowl of hot soup and an orange.

Fan sees me and smiles. "I missed you."

"I was sick yesterday."

"I know. Your teacher told me."

I swallow the soup. "I feel better now."

"Soup is good," she says, watching me eat. "My mother's chicken soup is the best."

"My mother makes soup too."

"You speak very well now. Better than before."

"That's because you are a good teacher," I say.

Fan smiles. "I wish I could be a real teacher."

"Maybe you can."

Fan sighs. "For a migrant, there are not many choices." She watches me slurp the soup. "Most Chinese girls that visit here from America are adopted. They've come to see their first home. And they don't know any Chinese at all." She picks up a section of the orange and chews it slowly. "You are a different kind of American girl. So what is it like in America?"

I'm not sure how to answer. In some ways, China is

really different from America. In the United States, the streets are not crowded like China, where they are full of people and bicycles and cars and buses going every which way. But in some ways, it's the same. Friends visit each other in their homes. If Fan comes to our house in Cincinnati, my mom will give her a bowl of steaming noodle soup.

"There are lots of big houses," she says.

I nod.

"How many rooms do you have?"

I count in my head. "Seven, not counting the bathroom."

"I see that in the movies." She looks down, then back up at me. "Do you think you are Chinese or American?"

I don't know what to say. When kids in the United States stare at me, I feel Chinese. When I am in the taxi in China and I cannot understand what the driver is saying, I feel very American. And when I am sitting on a park bench in China or on the floor at a CAT meeting, I feel . . . just like me. "Both," I say.

"That's good," she says. "Two is better than one."

Suddenly I have an idea. "Can I interview you for a school project?"

"I am not somebody important," she says quickly.

"You are my teacher and my friend in China," I say. "That is important."

"What do you want to know?" she asks.

"Can you tell me about the place where you used to live?"

Fan speaks slowly so I can understand most of her words. She grew up in a village many hours away from Beijing. She came to the city with her parents so they could work and earn money to send to their parents and other relatives. "I want to study someday," she says. "But it is difficult for migrants."

"What is a migrant?"

"A person who is not from Beijing."

"What do you want to study?" I ask.

"I like to study poetry," she says. "Chinese poetry."

I try to take notes in English, but I keep sticking Chinese words in. I can always translate them later.

"What do you like to do in your free time?"

She smiles. "I like to go out with my friends. We walk around and we talk."

"I like to talk to my friends too," I say. Suddenly I want to show her the paper fortune cookies from Andee. "Wait," I say. "I want to show you something." I run up and get the blue envelope.

"So funny," she says, reading each fortune. "Your friend is clever."

I explain to her about fortune cookies in America. I'm not sure if she understands. "When you come to America, I'll show you."

She glances at the clock on the wall. "I have to go now."

"Can I take a picture of you?" I ask.

She smooths her hair. Then I realize I left the camera in my room. "Here, you can take it on my phone and I'll send it to you."

"Thank you," I say, holding her phone and snapping a picture.

In the afternoon, we go to buy gifts for everyone in

the United States. Ms. Sylvester carries Baby Jing in a front carrier and we wander up and down the rows of little kiosks that line the streets. Mr. Sylvester buys key chains for his coworkers, and Ms. Sylvester buys baby books for Jing. I decide to get slippers with bunnies on them for Kaylee. For Ken, I get a kite that we can put together and fly from the top of the hill by the playground.

For Mom and Dad and Grandma I get their favorite Jasmine tea.

What should I get for Camille and Laura and Andee? There are blouses with embroidered collars and small purses and endless rows of key chains. Finally I see small notebooks with embroidered covers. I get Laura one with dogs, since she's crazy about them. For Camille I decide on one that has the character for "happiness" on the front. But what about Andee? I still don't know her that well, so I don't know what she would like. Then I see one with two children, one tall and one short, which reminds me of Andee and her mentee. I hand the three notebooks to the vendor.

"*Wu kuai qian*," she says. Five kwai.

I give her the money and she hands me the gifts.

Jing is sound asleep in the front carrier with her little head flopped forward and her hair sticking up.

"She's so cute," I say.

"Hard to believe that this is our last day in China," Ms. Sylvester says. "I feel kind of sad that we're leaving."

"Me too," I say. "I miss everyone at home so much, but when we leave, I will miss China."

"One thing I won't miss is the coffee," Mr. Sylvester says.

"Oh, Roy." Ms. Sylvester looks around. "I feel like . . . I feel like this is Jing's first home, and we are taking her away from it."

Jing opens her eyes for a minute, looks around, and then closes them again. I pat her head.

When we get back to our hotel room, I sit down on my bed and write a note to Fan:

Dear Fan,

I am so sad to say goodbye to you.
My home address is 3926 South Meadow
Street, Cincinnati, Ohio 45229. You have my
email address in your phone. Thank you very
much for being my teacher and my friend
and my big sister in China. I hope that
someday you can visit me, and that someday
I will come back to China to visit you
with my family.

Yours,
Anna Wang

Then I borrow Ms. Sylvester's scissors and cut out a circle. On a slip of paper I write a message.

I stick the fortune into the paper cookie and fold it shut.

We will see each other again.

Chapter Nineteen
Goodbye to China

The hotel lobby is crowded with all the couples and babies and suitcases. The guide is trying to shout above the noise.

"The van is waiting," she says. "Please give your suitcases to the man and take your seats."

I look around the lobby for Fan, but she is not there. Maybe she is off today, or she has a later shift. I should have told her we were leaving early in the morning. I give the paper fortune cookie and my note to the lady at the front desk and ask her to give them to Fan when she comes to work. As I talk, I realize that the words come easily in Chinese now, but I feel choked up. I am

about to get into the
van when I hear
someone calling
my name.

"Anna, Anna,
wait." Fan runs
up to me and
hands me a bag.
"For you. And for
your family."

"I was looking
for you," I say. "I
left you something."

Fan grabs my hand. "Come back soon."

"Hurry," the guide says. "We have to leave in one
minute."

I squeeze Fan's hand.

I follow the Sylvesters into the van and take a seat
by the window. Outside, Fan is waving, and I am waving back. The driver turns on the engine and we pull
away from the curb. I feel my eyes get watery.

❋ ❋ ❋

Inside the bag are four coloring books, a small pad of multicolored paper, a bag of candy, and a note in English. *Dear Anna, I hope this books can help with your Chinese. Share with your sister and brother. Good bye from China. Fan.*

I wipe the van window with my sleeve. We pass cars and trucks and bicycles and people bundled against the wind. I could be one of them, a Beijing girl walking to school or to the park or taking the bus to Fan's house. But now I am going home.

Ms. Sylvester puts her arm around me. "Thanks for coming with us, Anna."

"*Xie Xie*," Mr. Sylvester says.

Then we see that Baby Jing is holding up her hand and wiggling her fingers. "I think she is waving," Mr. Sylvester says.

"She is saying goodbye to China," I say.

The Sylvesters and Baby Jing fall asleep as soon as the plane takes off. I look through my journal entries from the past two weeks. Thirteen days is not a long time, and there are still lots of blank pages in the journal. What will I write in it once I get home? Or maybe I'll wait until my next trip to China, with Mom.

I lean back against the seat. What exactly will I do for the oral history project? I can write what I know about Fan, but she did not really tell me enough for a whole presentation.

I start doodling on the page. I sketch Baby Jing as she sleeps in her carrier. Her head is flopped back and her cheek is smashed against Ms. Sylvester's arm. I draw the airplane windows and the seats ahead of us. I have no idea how to actually do this oral history thing. Camille is right. It's harder than I thought. I wish I could call her right now. And Andee, too.

The plane ride is getting bumpy. Jing has her thumb in her mouth, and when the plane jerks, she sucks it a little. I wonder if she misses the orphanage with all the babies and the ladies who sang her songs and the up-and-down sounds of Chinese all around. But she seems happy with the Sylvesters. Maybe she forgot all that already.

Maybe I can do my oral history project about more

than one person. I can talk about Fan and the orphan-age ladies and the babies too. Nobody really knows the stories of the babies, and they are too small to tell them. Maybe I can write what I learned.

Jing wakes up and cries. Ms. Sylvester picks her up, but she doesn't stop. "I wonder what she wants?" Ms. Sylvester asks, checking her diaper, which is still dry.

I give Jing a rattle, but she's not interested. Mr. Sylvester gives Jing his keys. She shakes them for a while, but then she drops them and starts crying again.

"Maybe she's cold," I say, feeling the cool air that is blowing from the ceiling of the airplane. I reach into my backpack for the last hat. "When I went to the orphanage, one of the hats got stuck in my backpack," I say. I pull it onto Jing's head. "Now you match all the other babies," I tell her.

"The other babies?" Mr. Sylvester asks.

"The babies at the Lucky Family Orphanage," I say.

"They're kind of like Jing's sisters," Ms. Sylvester says. She closes her eyes. "Maybe she misses them."

Jing puts her arm up, feels the hat, and pulls it off.

I put it back on again. She pulls it off. She starts giggling as if this is the funniest game in the world.

I look at the map on the screen in front of me. We have a long flight ahead. The plane will land in Tokyo in about four hours, and in New York City eleven hours after that. When we finally get to Cincinnati, it will be tomorrow at seven in the evening. Mom and Dad and Ken and Kaylee and Grandma will be at the airport. I wish I could just close my eyes and be home.

Outside the sky is grayish white. I look down, but I can't see much because of the clouds. I start to write:

Oral History Project
Introduction

Now I am on the plane on my way back from China. I'm so glad that at the last minute, I finally got permission to visit my sister's orphanage. I delivered the knitted hats that were made. The caregivers were so happy! And I helped the Sylvesters with Baby Jing, and I saw lots of famous places around Beijing. My Chinese got better every day. I even made friends with Fan, a waitress in the hotel where we stayed. She took me to her home, which is one room that she shares with her parents and brother. But I think the most important thing was sitting on a park bench and realizing what it means to be Chinese.

I stop writing and look around. Baby Jing is snuggling in her mom's lap. Her dad has his arm around her mom. An ordinary family. Actually, I have no idea what it means to be Chinese, because it means something different to everyone: to Baby Jing and my sister and Ken and Camille and Andee and Fan and Mom and Dad. Being Chinese depends on so many little things that are impossible to separate. I cross out the last line and write:

I realize that being Chinese means something different to each person. To me it means not standing out. In China, nobody stared at me when I walked around, and I really liked that. But if I had lived all my life in China, I would never know what it feels like to look different. I think that's important because everybody feels different sometimes.

The clouds are moving past the windows of the plane. Even though we're traveling fast, they look soft and slow, but maybe from the ground, they are rushing by. I keep writing:

In China I realized that being Chinese is very important to me but so is being American and speaking English and living in my house with Mom and Dad and Ken and Kaylee and Maow Maow. I like making a snowman with Laura and talking to Camille before the bell rings and planning CAT projects with Andee and Sam and Simone.

I look up and see the backs of the heads of all the

people sitting in front of me on the plane. Some of them have Chinese babies and some don't. Some look mixed race and some don't. Some are tall and some are short, some are sleeping and some are awake.

I write:

I realize that I am a very lucky person.

I close my notebook. Then I remember that I have one last fortune cookie, which is silver: There is a small picture of a Christmas tree with presents underneath it. I almost forgot about Christmas.

I have many hours to make paper fortune cookies for everyone back home: Mom, Dad, Ken, Kaylee, Grandma, Camille, Laura, Andee, Sam, Simone, Ms. Remick, Mrs. Smith, Teacher Zhao. I don't have scissors, but I can start by making up the fortunes:

Mom: You will visit your family in China soon.
Dad: You will graduate from college this year.
Ken: Your Lego robot is the best!
Kaylee: You have a new friend named Jing.

Later I'll finish all the fortunes, copy them onto slips of paper, and fold them into paper cookies. But now I'm too sleepy to do anything except look out the win-

dow. Could that blue be a tiny glimpse of the ocean? I shut my eyes and think of home.

12. Cool in mini muffin tins to hold shape until crisp.
13. Repeat with remaining batter.

Read more at www.food.com/recipe/fortune-cookies -110768?oc=linkback.

The Year
of the Three Sisters

When Anna's friend Fan comes to the United States as part of a cultural exchange program, Anna knows that it won't be an easy adjustment. After her experience in China, Anna understands cultural differences; she expects Fan to feel homesick and to struggle with English. But the challenges that Anna faces with Fan and her other friends are not what she anticipates.

A Reply

$\mathcal{E}$very morning I check the email, but there is no reply from Fan. Finally on Monday morning, I see her name in my inbox.

Dear Anna,
Thank you very much to you and your friend for
invite me and offer to buy my ticket,
but I cannot come. I don't tell my mother
and father. They don't leave Beijing and
I go to America? But I dream about it every day.
I am tired from my job now.
Good bye and thank you very much for think
about me.
Your friend, Fan

My stomach drops. Fan's note is so short. She doesn't say that she will try to find a way to visit someday or that she got the letter from Mom. She doesn't write a poem or send a Chinese lesson. Did our invitation hurt her feelings in some way? At first I wasn't sure about the whole idea of inviting Fan to America, but now that she has said no, I feel so disappointed.

I call Andee and read her Fan's note over the phone. She doesn't say anything for so long that I wonder if we got disconnected. "Can you come over?" she asks finally.

"I have to babysit this morning. I'll see if my dad can bring me later."

When I get to Andee's house, she shows me earrings she is making out of shells that she found on the beach at Cape Cod. "You should get your ears pierced," she says.

"I hate needles," I say. "Even allergy shots."

"Let's make bracelets." Andee turns to face me. "I think Fan should at least have asked her parents."

Andee doesn't seem to understand that in China, helping your family is the most important thing in your life. I pick black, blue, and green thread to make a bracelet for Camille. "Maybe Fan was embarrassed to ask. To her family, going to America must sound completely impossible."

Andee is listening hard with her head tilted, the way she always did at the CAT meetings. "Are you . . . Do you think there's a still a chance that she could come?"

"My mom wrote a letter to her mom," I say. "I'm not sure if it got there yet." Andee is braiding red, pink, and white thread. Her fingers are long and agile, and the sun is shining on her hair. "I think it could make a difference."

"Anyway, Fan might not even show the letter to her parents," Andee says.

"The letter is to her mom. I think she will show it to her."

Andee takes a deep breath. "If Fan can't come, my mom said we could apply to host a regular Chinese exchange student through AFS."

Maybe Andee doesn't really care who comes as long as she has someone. We finish our bracelets without saying much.

Then Andee shows me two possible guest

rooms for the exchange student, a bigger one that faces the front of the house and a smaller one in back. Both rooms have their own bathroom attached.

"If Fan ends up coming, could she share your room? In China, she shares a room with her whole family."

"Don't you think she'd want some privacy?" Andee asks.

I shake my head. "She's used to having people around all the time."

We go back into Andee's room. "There isn't really that much space in here," she says, even though her room is big. "I guess she could use the art spot, and I could move my earrings and art stuff into the guest room."

We spend the afternoon cleaning up the alcove. We take all the art supplies into the guest room and move a bed from the guest bedroom into the art alcove. I think we should ask Andee's parents first, but she says that it's her room and she's allowed to rearrange things the way she wants. "What should we put on the wall?" she asks.

"In her room, Fan has posters of flowers and Chinese movie stars." I try to think of what else we could do. "It needs something colorful."

Andee gets out a stack of origami paper. We write *Welcome* in English and *Huan ying* in Chinese on red sheets.

欢迎

Then we look on the Internet to find the words for *welcome* in other languages and copy them as best we can onto different-colored pieces of paper. By the time

Dad comes to pick me up, the alcove is full of international floating Welcome signs.

When we pull up in front of the house, Mom runs out to the car. "Anna, your friend just called from China. I talked to her mother. She said they were so happy to read my letter, and that if Mrs. Wu can arrange everything, they will allow Fan to come!

Looking for a good mystery?

Discover the world of

Adventure and fun await

in the world of *Just Grace*